OBSESSION

Theophilia St. Claire

Nick has a hard life. Not only is he working at an East Harlem bar to make ends meet and pay for his sister's medical expenses, he's also on the run from a shady past that's surely catching up to him.

Most people think Claude has it easy due to the money and luxury surrounding him. But they would be wrong. Firmly trapped beneath his stern father's thumb, Claude's pre-determined life took a nosedive when his lover, Christian, left him a year ago.

When the two meet, sparks do not instantly fly between them. Claude thinks Nick is his ex-lover returned to him. Nick thinks Claude is crazy.

However, circumstances bring these two men together. And despite Claude's jealousy and possessive nature, Nick is falling for him. Sick of being mistaken for Claude's ex, Nick is willing to find out what happened to him—the real Christian. He'll have to if he wants a stable relationship with Claude. How Claude takes the truth, however, is the only thing that scares him.

A NineStar Press Publication

Published by NineStar Press
P.O. Box 91792,
Albuquerque, New Mexico, 87199 USA.
www.ninestarpress.com

Obsession

ISBN: 978-1-947904-47-7

Printed in the USA
First Edition
December, 2017

Also available in eBook, ISBN: 978-1-947904-46-0

Warning: This book contains sexually explicit content, which may only be suitable for mature readers, scenes of graphic violence, rape, and murder, mentions of childhood sexual abuse, and depictions of kidnapping, captivity, and domestic abuse.

Dedication

This book is dedicated to my father, for my passion and his mercy. To my family, for their continued love and support. And to Mom. I can't believe I'm letting you read this.

Acknowledgements

I'd like to thank NineStar Press for choosing me and this story!

Also, a huge thank-you to my editors, Jason, Barbara, and April. You guys are amazing to work with.

I'd like to thank all the bloggers who have such wonderful writing and business advice. You have no idea how much you're helping this lurker out.

Big shout out to my role-playing buddies at Midnight Trinity, and especially to Jen, for giving me a fun, creative outlet for the last seven years.

Last, but not least, I'd love to thank my fans—past, present, and future. This story is for you.

Chapter One

"CHRISTIAN?"

Nick glared at the fingers on his arm, the grip tight enough to be offensive. His gaze crawled its way up to the owner's face. Handsome guy. Tall. European-looking with stylish dark-blond hair and piercing hazel eyes. He stared at Nick expectantly, waiting for his response. His full mouth parted slightly.

I'm at work, Nick reminded himself. He couldn't go off on a rude customer again. Not if he wanted to keep his job. Nick shrugged off the stranger's grip. "Sorry, no." He carried the empty water pitcher through the lively crowd toward the bar.

His best friend, Eric Ruiz, raised a brow at him. "What was that about?"

"No clue. He called me Christian."

Eric frowned, stroking his goatee. "Christian? What? The name or the religion?"

"Do I care?"

"Sounds like a poor attempt at hollering at you, *hermano*." Eric sneered as he took in the customer's appearance. "Upper East Side boys ain't got no game."

Nick glanced over his shoulder, back at the table he'd just walked by. Even though he had company, the stranger focused on Nick. His expression hardened, dangerously so. "What the hell is his problem?"

"Don't worry about it, yo. Let's get back to work before Phil sees us slacking."

Nick agreed. Taking his thoughts away from the man, Nick headed off to check on his tables.

It was Valentine's Day, so Jenkins' Jazz Bar was busier than usual. Loving couples and groups of friends celebrating their singleness occupied every table and booth. Food and drinks flew from the kitchen at a rate almost too quickly to comprehend. Hell, Nick wasn't even sure the house band had taken a break yet. Since the bar opened that evening, it'd been one fast-paced blur.

Nick checked on a stylish older couple who should have been dining on Madison Avenue, not a basement joint in East Harlem.

That guy too, Nick thought. He stole a glance at table nine, which Mercedes tended. The stranger wasn't looking his way anymore, so Nick studied him a moment. The guy was groomed and decked out in top-notch designer clothes. Everything about him—from the way he sat to the way he sipped his cocktail—screamed money. He probably owned a penthouse on Fifth Avenue too. Nick gave a wry smile at the thought.

"We'll take two rum cakes. And I'd love another glass of this wine, if you don't mind."

Nick brought his attention back to the smiling woman. "Sure thing." He headed to the brand-new station to key in their orders.

The front door opened.

A young man wearing a black hoodie paired with loose-fit jeans stepped inside.

Nick sucked in a deep breath, inhaling the mingled scents of soul food. The visible tattoos on the guy's knuckles and neck did not bode well for Nick. Had they found him already? After only a year?

"Shit." Nick needed to check on two tables, but he didn't care about anything other than staying out of the guy's sight. He rushed into the kitchen, glad for the safety of the steel double doors.

"You okay? Look like you saw a ghost." Mercedes Shaw was the eighteen-year-old niece of Phil Jenkins, the bar's owner.

"Yeah," Nick replied. "Actually, you mind taking these rolls to table seven for me? I need a breather."

Mercedes's brown eyes softened with understanding. "Yeah, I got you. It's been like this all day, huh?"

Nick nodded, even though the fast pace wasn't the problem. He hurried out the back door with a sigh of relief.

The temperature had dropped into the low twenties, but the cold air soothed his flustered skin. Nick leaned against the building, raking a hand through his hair while trying not to think about the tattooed newcomer inside. Instead, he focused on his immediate surroundings, though there wasn't much to look at. The back door led to an alley that smelled like trash and piss. Police sirens and the occasional gunshot created life's soundtrack there in his corner of Manhattan. That, he was used to. He didn't want to give up the life he'd found there. Not yet. More than anything, he dreaded being back on the streets.

Nick didn't stay outside long. He wasn't looking to give Mr. Jenkins any reason to fire him. He just hoped the asshole had left already.

NICK'S SHIFT ENDED at one in the morning. Fortunately for him, the night flew by without further incident. Only the staff remained, bussing tables and cleaning floors, while the band put away their instruments and wiped sweat from their foreheads.

"Good job, everyone," Phil called out. He draped the towel onto his graying 'fro and glanced about the space with a hearty smile. "Boy, it's been a *long* time since I've played back-to-back like that. Stamina ain't what it used to be. I'm getting too old for this."

Nick nodded in agreement as he took a seat at the bar. He was only twenty-four, but all the running around had him feeling like a middle-aged man.

Eric set a shot of something in front of him. "You wanna stay at my place tonight?"

Nick barely peered up. He sifted through his tip money, calculating how much he needed for Amy's medical expenses and to get caught up on his rent. The night had been packed, but his tips were only marginally better than what he usually made on a good night. Most of the couples had probably bought expensive gifts first, then came out to dinner. Nick inwardly groaned. He was still short a few hundred dollars.

"Yo, Nicky. You ignoring me?"

"My bad." Nick grabbed the shot glass and downed the alcohol in one go. Tequila. He stuffed the money back into his pocket. "I'm just gonna go home. Coming with me to the bus stop?"

"Naw, I'm here 'til two. Inventory and shit. I'll see you tomorrow."

"Good luck with that." Nick gathered his things and left the bar.

Outside, the temperature had dropped from earlier, but the cold didn't faze Nick as he slid into his worn puffer coat. The bus stop was a half mile away on East 116th Street.

The darkness seemed heavy whenever Nick left work alone around that time. Sometimes, listening to music helped him not to notice the lack of streetlights in the area or imagine what lurked in the shadows, waiting to jump out at any moment. But he wouldn't be listening to anything, not after earlier. He pulled the hood of his coat on top of his head and tucked his hands into the pockets like he clenched something other than his MP3 player. He looked menacing, no doubt about it. The defense mechanism surprisingly kept him from being bothered most times.

Nick quickened his pace to the bus stop. He didn't enjoy being alone out there. Heavy footsteps followed closely behind Nick, noticeable without the sound of traffic. Nick glimpsed over his shoulder.

There, following a few feet behind him, was the tattooed gangster from earlier.

Nick's heart pounded. He almost stumbled as he continued to move forward, even while gazing backward.

The guy reached into his coat pocket.

Nick ran.

Chapter Two

CLAUDE SLID INTO his Ferrari with all the grace of a baby taking its first steps.

Jenkins' Jazz Bar had been the last place Claude would have chosen to meet with a business client. He rarely ever traversed that part of town, but Claude was required to oblige what the client requested. Showing up there, he hadn't expected much, certainly not the biggest surprise of the past twelve months.

Christian was back.

Unable to think clearly, Claude had stared upon his face, letting himself be assailed with memories. Christian's hair was shorter and darker than he remembered, but he hadn't forgotten those piercing green eyes that appeared pitch-black whenever angered.

He'd watched Christian long after his client had gone home. A part of him was relieved. Christian was all right. Claude had been worried for so long, though it appeared to have been for nothing.

The other part boiled with anger. Anger that Christian had walked away from him without a word. Anger that Christian had pretended not to recognize him.

Claude clenched the steering wheel. He wanted to hurt Christian for the pain, grief, and agony he'd cost him in the past year.

Several workers exited the bar for the evening, but Claude kept an eye out for Christian.

His cell phone rang. Claude answered without looking away from the dimly lit building. "What?"

"Mr. Vanderpoel?" It was Hannah Aldridge, his personal assistant. "I just received a call from Mr. Leibowitz. He's interested in doing business with us, sir, and he's put in quite a large order."

Well now, that was fast.

"Fax me the details. I want our best contractors handling Mr. Leibowitz's request first thing tomorrow morning."

"Yes, sir."

"Is there anything else?"

"No, sir, that's all. Have a good night."

Claude hung up in time to witness a hooded male exit the bar. Though too dark out to tell, he knew it was Christian. Every synapse in his body came alive at the thought.

Putting his car into drive, Claude followed him at a snail's pace with the headlights off.

Christian moved quickly along the sidewalk, as if anxious to get somewhere. Where was he headed? Claude wanted to know about the sort of life Christian had been living since they'd last seen one another. Shocking still was the fact Christian had gotten himself a job. He'd never held one in the years they'd been together.

All of a sudden, Christian took off at a dead run.

As he rounded the corner onto Pleasant Avenue, a man followed not too far behind him. He appeared to be struggling with something in his pocket.

Claude's gaze narrowed at the scene. He reached into the glove compartment for his firearm, a Walther P22 with a silencer. Although upset by Christian's betrayal and confused by his sudden reappearance, Claude would never allow anyone to hurt him.

He would die first.

Claude sped up to catch them. He drove beside the thug, who had yet to take notice. Rolling down the window, Claude took aim and fired.

The thug dropped with a pain-filled cry.

Christian spun around, his gaping mouth the only clue Claude needed to perceive his thoughts.

Claude parked beside him. "Get in the car."

Christian hesitated, but after glancing at the injured man struggling to his feet, he obeyed. Even in the silent darkness of Claude's car, Christian trembled visibly.

"Are you hurt?" Claude asked, visually checking him for any injuries. Besides his frazzled appearance, he seemed unharmed.

Christian shook his head. "No, I—I'm okay."

Claude nodded. He glanced out the window, only to note the thug had limped off somewhere. He stepped outside. "Wait here."

He was going to make sure the bastard never threatened Christian again.

Not waiting for a response, Claude chased after him. Cold air and the scent of car exhaust filled his lungs as he jogged up the street.

Claude wasn't entirely sure, but he believed the bullet hit the thug somewhere high on his leg. Maybe near his hip. He couldn't have gotten far.

It wasn't long before Claude spotted him making his way behind the Love Café. He wasn't exactly quiet, nor subtle. Most likely, he would try to gain attention from a patron in a nearby restaurant.

Claude sprinted after him. He knew he needed to put an end to this before someone saw them. Or worse, they crossed onto East 116th Street. Fortunately for him, the thug had disappeared beside the café, into the darkness.

Claude caught up with the limping man. He grabbed hold of his hooded jacket and shoved him onto a trash heap. The young man groaned in pain and clutched his upper thigh.

"Please, man. Let me go."

"Why were you chasing him?"

"Please, man. Please don't kill me." Disregarding Claude's query, the thug continued to babble incoherently, with tears spilling down his cheeks.

Claude put a bullet in his head.

Chapter Three

NICK WIPED HIS sweaty palms on his pants. His heart hadn't stopped pounding since he'd hopped into the car.

Who the hell was that guy?

More importantly, what did he want? Nick sank against the leather seat while he tried to figure out if the asshole who'd chased him had been sent. For all he knew, the guy could have been a petty thief who'd seen an opportunity and thought to take advantage of it. God knew there were enough homeless drug addicts in East Harlem who wouldn't hesitate at killing a man for their next fix.

Nick exhaled a breath he hadn't realized he'd been holding. Tension melted away, but it did nothing to alleviate his worries. He was alone in a strange car in the middle of a darkened street with a man who potentially wanted to kill him out there somewhere close.

Nick checked the ignition for the keys. They were gone. He checked the dashboard. A pair of expensive Ray-Bans and a shiny Patek Philippe watch that probably cost a small fortune sat there. Nick blinked twice, finally allowing himself to calm down enough to notice his surroundings more clearly. The car was a Ferrari. A newer model. Whoever his savior was, the guy was loaded. Nick frowned. He couldn't even picture the man's face. He'd been so afraid of being killed in retaliation, everything else had faded into the background. The only thing Nick remembered was a stern but smooth voice talking to him. Eloquent. Maybe even with an accent.

Nick popped open the glove compartment. A Louis Vuitton wallet tumbled into his lap. He didn't think twice about looking inside. Platinum credit cards and a wad of crisp cash greeted him. He couldn't remember the last time he'd seen that much money at once. Nick glanced at his savior's driver's license photo. His savior: the European-looking man from the bar. The one who'd called him Christian. His name was Claude Vanderpoel and he lived on Fifth Avenue.

"I called it," Nick mumbled.

Claude was also only twenty-eight years old.

Nick put everything back the way he found it. He hoped he had his shit together by the time he reached Claude's age.

A moment later, the driver's door opened. Claude slid inside and locked them in together.

Nick tensed. Physically, Claude wasn't much bigger than him. Probably two or three inches taller, and maybe packing a little more muscle beneath his clothes. But for some reason, Nick was...intimidated.

Claude's presence loomed over him like some superior force while he regarded him quietly with laser-like eyes prodding through Nick's exterior.

Nick cleared his throat. "Did you find him?"

"Don't worry. That man won't be threatening you again."

Where Nick came from, that usually meant the person was dead. He didn't have the gall to ask Claude if he'd killed his assailant. Especially since Claude carried around a gun he wasn't afraid to use.

Claude scanned him over once more before putting the car into drive. "The police will find him."

Nick nodded. "Could you take me to the bus stop? It's right up here on 116th." He'd give away his least favorite appendage to be home, putting that entire night behind him.

"No. It's not safe."

"What?" Nick arched a brow. Had he heard him correctly?

"You'll be safer with me. I'm taking you home."

Nick stiffened. "You know where I live?"

"No," Claude said through clenched teeth. "And as dismaying as that is, I meant that I'll be taking you to my apartment."

Though Claude seemed agitated, Nick didn't care. He wanted out of that car. No way he was going with that guy to his place or anywhere. "I don't think so, pal. Stop the car."

"Don't be ridiculous."

"Stop the fucking car now." Nick preferred not to walk alone after what'd happened, but he didn't trust Claude's eagerness to get him to his place. Maybe he should text Eric, find out how close he was.

Claude pulled the car to a stop in front of the Love Café. Nick pushed the passenger door open. Before he could leave, Claude grabbed his arm, his expression a mixture of sadness and displeasure.

Nick shook his head in confusion. What the hell was that guy's deal?

"I'll take you wherever you need to go. Just don't leave again." Claude stared at him, unblinking and unmoving while waiting for a response.

Nick met his gaze for all of ten seconds before he directed his sight toward the orange overhang on top of the café's dark exterior. "Fine." He closed the door again, glad when the inside warmth swallowed the cold air. "The bus stop up ahead."

They rode the short drive in silence. On the way, Nick thought about the things he'd learned about Claude, a man he'd been curious about since their first encounter back at the bar. Outside of the whole gun thing, the one detail Nick kept coming back to was the fact Claude was loaded. And Nick was short a few hundred dollars.

Don't do this, Nick...

Nick scrubbed at his face. What would it be like to go home with Claude? To do what he used to do for money before he chose to leave behind his old life?

Claude parked his Ferrari beside the bus stop. "I'm not sure when the bus arrives, but I'll wait here until you board safely."

Nick gazed out the window. There were a few others waiting. Two young women dressed scantily despite the cold, though the way they clutched their purses in their lap, they might be packing. A Latino man in a hoodie blabbed away on his cell phone in Spanish. Nick recognized a few of the insults. The trio eyed the car.

Claude unlocked the door, but Nick didn't move. He squeezed his eyes shut. "Take me to your place." He hoped he wasn't making a big mistake.

CLAUDE'S "APARTMENT" ENDED up being a huge penthouse in a skyscraper building on Fifth Avenue.

Just as he'd called.

The concept was open floor plan with a house theme of black, charcoal gray, and glass. Lots of glass. The floors were black-veined marble. Nick surveyed the living room, slack-jawed at its leather sectional and recliner and frosted-glass tables—one of which stood behind the sofa, with an expensive-looking black vase filled with white oleanders. A sixty-inch plasma television was mounted on the wall in its own niche above a cozy electric fireplace with an ornate black gate.

"You got this whole floor to yourself?" Nick asked.

"The entire floor, but you knew that." Claude disappeared into the kitchen.

"I pretty much guessed it." Nick followed him, his gaze landing on the large crystal chandelier hanging above the fancy dining room table. Claude's home was easily the most expensive place he'd ever been inside. The kitchen was a gourmet chef's dream, what with all the black and stainless steel appliances.

"Are you hungry? I have some parmesan chicken pasta from last night." Claude pulled open the damned near industrial-size refrigerator and retrieved a silver container.

Nick took a seat on one of the heather-gray stools at the island. He tried not to fidget with his hands. "I'm starving, actually."

Claude wasted no time serving up a hot helping to Nick in a decorative glass plate. It smelled divine, like cheeses and herbs. Nick shoved a forkful into his mouth with a satisfied moan. Though they were leftovers, the pasta still tasted fresh. The meat was tender.

"This is good. You make this yourself?"

"Yes." Claude filled two champagne glasses with red wine. He handed one to Nick. "Do you want to tell me why that man was chasing you?"

Nick swallowed the food in his mouth. He kept his gaze lowered to the black granite countertop while he sipped the smooth wine. It tasted like plums and strawberries. "You'll have to ask him. I don't know."

"You don't know him?"

"No, I don't." Nick ate another forkful of the pasta. The second bite wasn't as good as the first.

Claude retrieved a silver cigarette case from his pocket. Placing a loose one between his lips, he lit up and inhaled deeply. The scent of exotic spices and earth drifted in the space between them.

Usually Nick hated the smell of cigarettes, but that wasn't like anything he'd ever smelled before. "What is that?"

Claude exhaled a cloud of white smoke away from him. "This is one hundred percent Turkish tobacco. Not the American blend you find here."

"Smells good."

Claude eyed him a long moment with heat dilating his pupils. Nick knew what he wanted. He'd seen the look too many times.

He finished his food in five minutes flat and drained the remainder of his wine. "Thanks for the meal."

"You're welcome," Claude mumbled. He took Nick's dishes and placed them in the dishwasher.

"Could I use your bathroom?"

"Down the hall."

"Thanks." Nick headed there, admiring the modern chic décor he passed by. He'd always wanted a similar place for himself. Maybe with some more color, of course. The monochromatic scheme wasn't bad, though. Oddly enough, he found it suitable for Claude.

Nick found the guest bathroom, filled with white marble, polished chrome, and glass. He shut himself inside and twisted the shower dial. While the water heated, he stripped out of his uniform.

He took a deep, calming breath.

It'd been a long time since he'd done this. And never with anyone remotely equal to Claude—a man so powerful, successful, and direct. No one he'd ever hooked up with had been as eloquent or handsome as him, either. Hopefully, the shower soothed his nerves.

The stream of water was blessedly hot when he stepped inside, instantly relaxing the tension in his muscles. Nick reclined his neck backward, letting the water rain on his face. He'd missed hot water. At his apartment, water got tepid at best, and it didn't last long.

Even though he wanted to live in there, Nick cleaned himself with the expensive bodywash and shampoo available. He dried off and wrapped the towel around his waist.

Nick went looking for him.

Though the penthouse was pretty large, he didn't take long to find Claude in the master bedroom. It was the only door opened wide. Inviting. Nick studied Claude from the doorway. He'd taken off his shirt and worked on removing his belt.

Nick's cock twitched at the sight of all that tawny, muscled skin. He cleared his throat.

Claude glanced over his shoulder, pausing at the sight of him. He licked his lips.

Nick took the gesture as his invitation to come inside. "I hope you don't mind I took a shower." Nick browsed around. The master bedroom alone was bigger than his apartment. The walls were floor-to-ceiling windows with a panoramic view of the lit city and Central Park. A king-size bed with black silk sheets and pillows was perched on a raised marble platform. A black bureau stood beside the bed, and on the other side of the room sat another beautiful fireplace. A lighted tray ceiling with an elegant chandelier hovered above him. The room smelled faintly of cologne and the cigarettes Claude had smoked earlier. Nick headed straight for the windows.

"Of course not," Claude answered, his voice octaves lower.

Nick splayed his fingers across the glass, staring out at the view. He'd walked the streets of New York City for years, never understanding the hype from his vantage point down there. Up high, though...it was pretty majestic. Everything below resembled a jeweled spectacle.

The room was suddenly plunged into darkness. Nick didn't move. Heat from Claude's body engulfed him as he stood behind him. The towel slid off his waist. Nick sucked in a deep breath.

Claude's hands were steady as they glided across Nick's chest, down his abs, and finally took hold of his semi-erect cock. Claude sucked his earlobe between his teeth.

"I missed this," he whispered.

Nick moaned. He didn't want to speculate what Claude meant by that. Hell, he could barely think straight with Claude's deft hand sliding up and down his shaft. Nick didn't remember any of his clients ever trying to make him feel this good. No, they usually couldn't wait to throw him on the seedy motel beds and get their money's worth.

Meanwhile, Claude made his blood boil with his sensuous caresses and soft kisses to his heated skin.

Nick arched into his hand, wanting more. More stroking. More touching. More everything.

Claude spun him around. It wasn't difficult to see his face with the moon at Nick's back. Nick swallowed as he peered into that hard, indiscernible gaze. He couldn't guess what Claude was thinking, but the way he stared at him...like he was soaking him in. Burning him into memory.

Nick squirmed.

Claude cupped his cheek. "Are you nervous now?"

Yes. "No," Nick lied.

"Good." Claude pressed their lips together.

Nick didn't hesitate to return the kiss. Claude's lips were soft and tender. He tasted like spice and scotch. And danger. The way he kissed Nick with so much passion and heat made Nick feel less like a cheap male whore and more like the most desired man in all of New York City.

Claude pushed him face-first against the cool glass. "Wait here." He placed a chaste kiss between Nick's shoulder blades before leaving him.

Nick's stomach knotted in anticipation. He contemplated the city through half-mast eyes, wondering if anyone could see him—legs spread and body ready to be fucked by a stranger for money. And if someone were looking at him, even from this height, would they know what he was?

Claude's fingertips sliding across his butt brought him back into the moment. Claude made shuffling movements behind him before sighing deeply, likely after he tore open a condom wrapper and slipped the rubber on.

Nick licked his lips. Claude drizzled lube on his ass. He worked the cold, wet substance into him with his fingertips until Nick dripped precum.

Claude buried his face against Nick's shoulder, raining kisses to his bare flesh. "Relax. I'm going in."

Nick nodded. He braced himself.

The first thrust was slow and painful. Nick clenched his teeth hard enough to hurt his jaw. Claude was hot and so thick, he filled him completely. It'd definitely been a while since Nick had done this with anyone.

Claude nudged apart his legs farther and bent him slightly. A satisfied groan escaped him as he pushed deeper inside.

"Jesus," Nick moaned. Claude slid in and out of him with controlled, deep strokes. Nick's sweltering breaths fogged up the glass as he rocked his hips to Claude's smooth cadence.

Claude easily took the lead, touching and stroking him, positioning him around for optimal gratification.

Meanwhile, Nick's head spun, dizzy with pleasure. His body was so hot, he thought he might have a fever. The dark, musky scent of their sex was intoxicating. Nick's mouth was suddenly dry.

As if reading his mind, Claude repositioned Nick's head until their mouths met.

Nick moaned into him.

"Are you ready to come, *mijn lief?*"

Nick nodded. He probably looked crazy in that moment, his chin wet with saliva and his eyes glazed. He didn't care. He'd never felt so good in his entire life. So treasured. Only Amy filled him with any kind of warmth, but that was different. Claude made him hot. The way he handled Nick as he kissed him and thrust into his body made Nick think of a considerate lover. Not at all like they were strangers who'd met a few hours before.

Nick's breathing grew erratic. He reached behind him, needing to hold something. Anything. His hands met with a fistful of Claude's hair. He gripped the dark-blond locks, thrusting back in sync with Claude's strokes.

"Gonna come," he exclaimed. The sounds of their moans and pants, their skin slapping one another's while they fucked, grew louder and more intense.

"Good. Let's go together."

"Fuck." Nick squeezed his eyes shut. He strained and cried out as jets of hot semen spurted from him.

Behind him, Claude shuddered and released a long-held breath as he filled the condom.

Nick slumped to the floor in a panting mess, but Claude caught him. He picked Nick up bridal-style and carried him to the bed.

Nick would be offended if he wasn't so exhausted.

The silk was heaven on his skin. He eyed the elaborate ceiling, even though his lids grew heavy.

Claude pressed a damp cloth against his cock. Nick shivered as his sensitive bits tingled. He hadn't realized Claude left the room. Once he finished wiping him clean, Claude pulled Nick against him, his back to his chest, and entwined their legs together.

Nick stiffened. He'd never been spooned before.

Claude kissed his head. "I missed you."

NICK DIDN'T SLEEP long. No matter where he was, he had a hard time falling asleep in unfamiliar places.

Two hours had passed. Claude was still sleeping, his arm thrown over Nick's side. Nick gently pried him off and settled at the edge of the bed, staring out the window. The sun had yet to break over the horizon, so the sky was still dark.

Nick gathered his clothes. They were actually washed and folded neatly on the black bureau. Once dressed, he peered at Claude, who still hadn't moved, and thought about what happened hours before. He bit his lip at the vivid memories. A part of him didn't want to go through with it. The guy had protected him, fed him, fucked him, and didn't seem to want anything in return.

But when he thought of the money he needed for Amy, Nick knew he didn't have a choice. He tried not to think about it while he rummaged through Claude's drawers of mostly underwear and some X-rated stuff. His fancy clothes were probably hung up in his huge walk-in closet. He spotted Claude's cigarette case, filled with his Turkish tobacco. Nick pocketed one. If he ever lit it, he hoped he'd remember the short but sweet time he shared with Claude.

In the last drawer, Nick found what he was searching for: a gold money clip holding together a wad of cash. All crisp one-hundred-dollar bills. Nick didn't bother counting. He took two hundred, refusing to let guilt creep up on him. That was just payment for last night, he told himself.

Nick left the penthouse and prayed he never saw Claude again.

Chapter Four

Claude was awake.

He'd been awake the entire time Christian had rifled through his things and stolen money from him. Once Christian had left, Claude hadn't been able to get out of bed to start his day properly.

"I guess some things never change," he said aloud.

Honestly, he didn't know why he was so surprised. That wasn't the first time Christian stole from him. Oftentimes in the past, his lover would steal cash and buy gifts for other men he'd taken a liking to.

It'd been foolish to hope that after all that time things would be different.

Claude sat up in bed, raking a hand through his hair. He finally noticed the scent of bacon, eggs, and roasted coffee. Vicky and Yesenia, his maids, had let themselves in without his knowing.

Damn Christian for clouding his mind like that.

Disappointed, Claude moved to shower and dress for the day. In the kitchen, he filled a thermos with black coffee before leaving his apartment.

Sundays were usually his day off to relax from a stressful workweek, but he slid into his Ferrari and headed to work anyway. He needed the distraction. Traffic wouldn't be too bad, and he'd have enough time to think about Christian.

Christian...

If last night was any indication, Christian obviously owed money to somebody. Who was the question. Had that thug been sent after Christian for what he owed?

Claude frowned in distaste. It wasn't Christian's status quo to deal with street rats.

Though a bit disappointed, Claude couldn't make himself be too upset. After all, Christian was back. It'd been too long, and last night had been a revelation.

Claude sped down the street right as the light changed red. He planned on seeing Christian soon. And this time, he wasn't ever letting him go.

Chapter Five

"YOUR ADMIRER IS inside."

"What?" Nick frowned at his best friend, Eric, and his stupid grin. He'd just interrupted his outside break.

"You know. Upper East Side from the other day, yo. The guy who was slick trying to holla at you."

"Fuck." Had Claude found out what he'd done already?

Eric folded his muscled arms across his thick chest. "What's he here for anyway? You talk to him?"

"Not exactly." Nick didn't meet his gaze. Instead, he trudged inside. The bar was only moderately packed. Low jazz music played in accompaniment with the mood created by the dim lights and nude/chocolate furniture.

Nick stayed in the back, peeking through the double doors until he spotted Claude. He sat alone in a booth, legs crossed, head tilted back as he scanned the bar. He didn't look too happy, either. Nick's heart pounded.

"Yo."

Nick nearly jumped at the sound of Eric's voice behind him. He'd forgotten his friend was there. "What?"

"What's going on with you and him anyway?"

Nick scowled in distaste. "Me and him? Nothing." He blocked off images of the other night from his mind. "On Saturday, this fucking guy tried to rob me on my way to the bus stop."

Eric gaped. "What the fuck?"

"I know, right? Some crackhead probably looking for money for his next hit or something," Nick lied. He couldn't tell Eric who his would-be attacker might *actually* be. His friend didn't know about his past life, and Nick intended to keep it that way. "Anyway, that guy out there, the one in the booth, he happened to be there to chase him off with a gun."

Eric laid eyes on him, his dark gaze unreadable. He stroked his goatee like he was deep in thought. "So it was you," he said.

Nick arched a brow at him. "What do you mean?"

"The pigs were in the area because someone had been attacked. They were arresting some thug."

Nick sighed in relief. "That must have been after I left."

"I guess. Anyway, why didn't you tell me?"

Nick shrugged and tied his apron around his waist. "It was no big deal. I went home after everything." He hated lying to Eric, but there was no way in hell he was telling him about where he'd gone and what he'd done with Claude. Just thinking about it made him feel dirty.

"You could've stayed at my place." Eric gave him a lecherous grin as he threw an arm around his shoulder. "I could've protected you."

Nick shrugged him off. "Vintage Eric Ruiz, always trying to get me to your place."

"Hey, I try."

"There you are."

Both of them glanced up the same time the double doors swung open. A flush-faced Mercedes strode toward Nick, hands on her slim hips. "There's a customer at table twelve who keeps asking for you. Says he won't accept another waiter."

Nick scrubbed his face and stared out the window. He didn't want anything to do with Claude, but maybe that was the perfect opportunity to apologize for what he'd done. He should have asked in the first place.

Mercedes continued, "And who the heck is Christian anyway? I kept telling him there's no waiter here by that name, but he wouldn't listen. I asked him to explain what this *Christian* looked like, and he described you, Nick. Did you lie to him about your name or something?"

"Don't worry about it. I'll deal with him." Nick pushed open the doors and marched into the front of the house. The music was louder there, though not loud enough to be disturbing. The smell of smothered pork chops, potatoes, honey ham, cheeses, and all other sorts of soul food made his nose itch as he passed by tables with customers in the middle of their meal.

His nerves tingled the closer he got to Claude. That same stern frown hadn't changed, even though Claude noticed him.

Nick stopped at his booth. He pulled out a pen and pad. "What can I get you?"

"Christian."

Nick frowned. "Why do you keep saying that? What exactly are you asking?"

Claude's golden-green eyes narrowed. "You're not funny."

"No, I'm not. I'm also not Christian, either. I haven't been Christian in a long time. Not really." He'd stopped praying to God the moment God stopped listening to him. "I'm Nick."

Claude gawked at him, confusion etched into his features.

"I'm sorry I stole from you," Nick blurted. "I promise to pay you back every dollar."

Claude waved his hand dismissively. "I don't care about that. I have money. Lots of it." He crossed his arms while practically boring a hole through Nick with his intense gaze. "What I'm curious about is why you took it in the first place? Who's the money for?"

Nick bit his lip. He never ever talked about his family with anyone, especially someone he'd fucked with no intention of seeing again. Still, he owed the man an explanation, and that was the only one he had.

"My little sister. She has leukemia. I need money to pay for her treatments because we don't have health insurance."

"I didn't know you have a sister."

Nick cleared his throat. The conversation was over. "So what can I get for you?"

"Come home with me tonight."

Nick bristled at the authoritative way he spoke, practically demanding him. Claude was definitely the type used to getting his way. Nick scoffed. "No thanks." He'd done enough self-flagellation. He didn't need to go down that road again. Not even for a night of incredible sex.

Claude frowned in exasperation. "You're telling me no again?"

Nick closed his pad and stuffed his pen behind his ear. "You can call me back when you're ready to order."

Chapter Six

"Mr. Vanderpoel, this came for you earlier."

Claude stopped on the way to his office to glance at his blonde assistant, Hannah Aldridge. She retrieved a three-piece stainless steel case from inside her desk.

Claude froze to the spot, his gaze riveted to the familiar box. He knew exactly what it held.

Though Hannah schooled her features into indifference, her brown eyes were filled with sympathy at his latest plight.

"Thank you, Hannah." Claude took the case from her. "Is that all?"

"Mr. Finch called. His wife's ill so he needs to reschedule his meeting. Also, Abri called. The bocote wood arrived last night for Mr. Leibowitz's boat."

"I want the contractors out there first thing tomorrow morning."

Hannah made a note of it. "Your father also called. He said he would like to set up a meeting with you soon as you're available."

Claude's shoulders stiffened. He had no interest in sitting with his father, and he planned to be as unavailable as possible. There were more pressing things on his mind then. "I'll be forwarding my calls to you."

"Yes, sir."

Claude shut himself inside his office. Alone in the dimly lit space with its modern-chic amenities, he allowed the boiling rage he'd been suppressing to reach its surface. Claude focused on the box, hoping it would be empty inside, though he knew it wasn't. The case was too heavy. He pried it open. The Zannetti Regent Dragon timepiece he'd purchased stared back at him. Claude's fingers brushed along the engraved Sapphire anti-reflex glass and the hand-stitched Louisiana alligator leather strap. The watch cost nearly seven grand.

Christian had sent it back.

Claude slumped into his seat. Nearly a week had passed since his initial offer, and since then, he'd made a point of sending gifts to Christian's workplace in an attempt to not only sway him, but to let him see Claude's feelings where he was concerned. He was no longer angry at Christian for leaving him a year before. In fact, he hoped to resume their relationship with no hard feelings.

Yet Christian had returned every single offering with no explanation. Claude was dumbfounded. Even if Christian wasn't looking to continue a relationship with Claude, he never turned away an expensive trinket. Especially if Claude paid for it.

Claude shut the watch inside his drawer, refusing to stew over it any longer. However, he'd begun to grow tired of Christian's stubbornness, and he planned to let him know it.

CHRISTIAN LEFT THE bar where he worked at nearly midnight.

Claude sat in his car across the street as his former lover pulled up the hood on his coat to protect himself from the bitter cold. Another man exited behind him. That one, Claude recognized. He was the Puerto Rican bartender.

The two laughed together as they walked down East 114th Street. A red haze filled Claude's vision. He jumped out of the car before he thought about it. "Christian!"

They noticed him. Though hard to tell their expressions, Claude imagined what they might be as they glared in his direction. He wasn't deterred in the slightest.

Christian said something to his friend that Claude couldn't hear. Though the bartender seemed reluctant to leave, he finally walked off on his own, much to Claude's instant relief.

He approached Christian, noticing the annoyance on his face. Claude positioned himself in front of the younger male. "I think you've avoided me long enough." He peered in the direction the bartender had gone. "Is he your new lover now?"

"Why are you here?"

"Why do you keep returning the gifts I send?"

"Because I'm not impressed with them. What? You think you can buy me or something?"

Claude frowned, genuinely perplexed by the hostility emanating from Christian. He hardly thought that at all. For as long as they'd been together, he'd always spoiled Christian with luxury items. He never asked for recompense, either. Only hope for Christian's loyalty and faithfulness to him. Claude wasn't there to argue semantics, however. If Christian didn't want them, there was nothing to be done about it.

"I want you to come home with me. Where you belong."

Christian didn't respond. Instead he reached into his coat pocket and pulled out a handful of crumpled bills. "I knew you would show up sooner or later." Christian shoved the money into Claude's palm. "Here. It's not two hundred, but I'll have the rest of it soon." Christian walked away from him.

Claude growled low in his throat. Every cell in his body begged him to go off on the boy. To pull him into the car and take him by force, then lock him away so he could never leave again.

He took a deep breath to calm himself. Being angry with Christian would get him nowhere. Christian never responded well to anger. Claude hurried after him and pulled him to a stop. He searched Christian's visage for signs of interest in rekindling the flame between them. There were none. Christian seemed as confused as he was.

Claude pulled the younger male into his arms and kissed him. His lips were cold and dry. Unwelcoming. Claude would give anything to explore them again. To make them hot and moist and swollen from his love.

"Why do you do this to me?"

Christian shoved him away. "I don't even know you," he shouted. Before Claude could say another word, Christian ran off.

Claude stood there, stunned, his chest aching. As much as the words pained him, he wouldn't let Christian go. Not when Claude finally had him within reach.

He got into his car and drove to East 116th Street in time for Christian to board the M102. He was unable to tell where exactly Christian sat, but Claude trailed the bus. He followed it for five stops until Christian got off at the Malcolm X Boulevard stop.

Christian kept his hood up, ignoring everyone else around him while he disappeared into the subway station. Claude stayed behind him a good distance as he took the Number 2 subway line to wherever.

Claude was familiar with the route. He knew the stops and time frame adequately. The farther he drove, the worse the area became. Poverty, high crime, and drug addiction were leading social problems in that corner of the world. Public housing units filled almost every block. Claude pitied the sad souls who called that place home.

He spotted Christian exiting the station on 96th and Broadway. He resembled a menacing figure with his hood down low over his eyes and clutching something in his pocket as if it was a gun. A pocketknife was more likely, though Claude could see how one would think he carried a firearm for protection. As he walked toward West 95th, Christian eyed his surroundings warily, as if waiting for someone to attack or mug him.

Claude surveyed his surroundings for an entirely different reason.

How could Christian possibly have made a living down there? Watching his back every second to make sure it wouldn't be stabbed? He passed by all manner of homeless people and shady characters. Trash littered the streets and graffiti covered multiple surfaces. Police sirens roared a few blocks away. The air reeked of filth. During their time together, Claude sometimes thought Christian needed to be taught a humbling lesson in economics. But he wouldn't choose this for him.

Christian entered an old, outdated public housing unit. Two police officers stood outside with several tenants. Claude shut off his engine. Christian slowed his brisk pace as an officer approached him. They spoke. Claude wasn't close enough to hear what they conversed about, but he knew the instant Christian grew upset. The boy went rigid. He stared in the direction of what Claude assumed to be his apartment in that godforsaken place. Christian broke into a sudden run up a short flight of stairs and disappeared into one of the apartments.

Claude's heart raced. He had no clue what was going on, but he needed to be there for Christian.

Stepping out of his car, Claude approached the same uniform who'd spoken to Christian. The man eyed him warily. "Stop right there, sir."

Claude stopped and made a show of holding out his hands so the man would see he was unarmed.

The officer looked him up and down, taking in his attire. He knew Claude did not belong there. "Sir, are you lost?"

Claude didn't have time for that. "I'm with a friend. He just ran into his apartment and I'm concerned for him."

"Oh." The officer relaxed a degree. "Poor kid. It's pretty bad up there."

"If you don't mind my asking. What happened?"

"Break in. Vandalism. Don't know if they took anything, but the perps were looking for something, that's for damn sure. I hope it's not drug-related. You deal with people like that and they'll do anything to get back what belongs to them. This was just a warning."

Claude nodded. He'd wondered the same thing the night the thug had chased Christian outside his workplace. Not only that, but Christian had stolen from him. Although he'd told Claude the money had been for his sick sister, it was obvious he'd been lying. Someone was after him. Some unsavory person likely involved with gangs and drugs.

"I'm going up to see him now."

The cop nodded. "Oh, by the way, tell your friend to make a list of what's missing, if anything. He also needs to go down to the station to make a statement. He ran off before I could say anything. Here's my number."

Claude took the card from him. "Thank you, Officer Finlay." He left before they asked anything else. It wasn't hard locating which apartment belonged to Christian. Of them all, his was the only one left wide open. Claude stepped inside and was floored by the sight. Besides the fact the tiny apartment desperately needed updating and a good thorough cleaning, the space had been destroyed. Clothes and trash were strewn about. Furniture lay in broken pieces. The thin walls were slashed through with a knife, so much so he could see into the neighbor's house. Food splatter decorated the entire kitchen. More broken glass.

In the midst of the chaos, Christian sat near the upended sofa with his back facing him, gazing at something Claude couldn't glimpse.

Claude approached. When he drew closer, he noticed Christian's trembling. Claude placed a careful hand on his shoulder. "Christian…"

"Look." Christian spun around to face him. Hatred darkened his features. Unshed tears filled his eyes as he glared at Claude. He held up a picture of a girl. A beautiful young girl with the word SLUT written in bold ink beneath her rounded chin.

"I'm sorry."

"Who would do this? What sick, twisted fuck would say this about a little girl?" Christian trembled even more, hysterical.

Not knowing what else to do, Claude wrapped his arms around Christian and held him. "It's all right now. I'm here." He kissed his head, hoping to comfort him. Despite his earlier words, Claude could never leave Christian when he needed him most.

Christian stiffened but didn't pull away. A good sign. Minutes ticked by. Possibly a half-hour's worth. Claude continued to hold him until he'd relaxed somewhat. "I'm taking you home with me tonight. You shouldn't be here alone."

Christian wiped at his red-rimmed eyes. "No. I need to call Eric."

"Eric?"

"I need to tell him what happened." Christian walked off. He retrieved the cell phone from his pocket and moved outside.

Claude closed his eyes, deliberately counting to ten while tamping down on the jealousy threatening to rear its head at the mention of the male name. He decided to take a look around. Inspect the damage. There were no bedrooms in the apartment, though there was a single full-size bathroom. Claude stepped inside. The bathroom was outdated with cheap blue-and-white tile and an old-fashioned claw-foot tub. Besides a few toiletries on the floor, the area was spotless. Though appalled by Christian's living conditions, Claude refused to show the expression when he joined Christian outside.

Christian shut off his phone and palmed his forehead. "I can't reach him."

"Is there anyone else you can call?"

"No."

"Will you stay with me tonight?"

Christian hesitated. "Yes."

CLAUDE WAS GLAD to be back home on Fifth Avenue. More than that, he was ecstatic to have Christian with him. As they rode the elevator up to his suite, Claude kept a protective arm wrapped around Christian's shoulders. He'd yet to let him go since they'd walked out of Christian's housing unit together.

The doors slid open and Claude led him inside. "Welcome back."

Christian glared at him but otherwise had no snarky comeback. He peeked around, clearly uncomfortable with his "new" surroundings.

"Let's put your things away." Claude reached for Christian's overnight bag, but Christian pulled back before he made contact.

"I want my own room," he stated.

"Of course you do."

"I'm serious."

Claude analyzed his hard stare, desperate to figure out Christian's feelings toward him. Why was he being so damned difficult? "All right. I'll give you your space. You can take the guest room if that's what you prefer."

"Thanks," Christian mumbled. He slunk off without another word.

Claude watched him go before he, too, disappeared into his office. He had much work to do...

It was nearly four in the morning when Claude undressed for bed. Throwing himself into work had been mind-numbing at best. The perfect distraction from the fact that Christian was back home, sleeping in the guest bed a few doors down.

Though he should be with me.

Still, it was a miracle to have him back. He would take that.

Claude pulled the silk sheet over his nude body when a soft knock sounded on his bedroom door. Claude rolled onto his side and eyed it. "Come in."

Christian pushed open the door. "Were you sleeping? If you were, I can come back—"

"No, I wasn't. Not yet. Come in."

Christian closed the door behind him. He approached the bed with hesitant, unsure steps.

Claude's gaze skimmed over Christian's lean figure clad only in a pair of boxers and a T-shirt. Claude's cock twitched. Christian had the type of body he preferred for his lovers.

Christian stopped a foot away from the raised platform. His breaths were shallow and unsteady. "I can't sleep. I can't stop worrying about everything." He paused. "I don't want to be alone right now."

Claude sucked in a deep breath. He knew where the conversation was headed.

Christian continued, "I need you to take my mind off this." He licked his lips. "Fuck me."

Claude groaned. Those two words sent a lance of heat straight to his penis. He'd forgotten how direct Christian could be. Claude pulled back the blanket, urging his younger lover to climb inside. When he did, Claude wrapped around him from behind, pressing the front of his body flush against Christian's back.

Christian moaned softly as Claude pressed against him.

"I swear I will. But first, let me hold you for a while." He wanted to savor that moment. That victory. At Christian's nod, Claude burrowed his face against his neck, inhaling the crisp scent of ginger-and-citrus body product. Claude couldn't help a big smile.

Christian needed him again.

Chapter Seven

NICK WOKE UP alone in bed. The curtains were pulled open, giving him a panoramic view of New York City in the daytime. He scrubbed his face.

Shit, he was at Claude's.

He'd been hoping last night had been a dream. Despite everything that'd happened at his place, Nick hadn't wanted to come home with Claude again. Not because of the sex thing, but because Claude's persistence freaked him out. Claude acted like they knew one another from a past life or something. Still, Nick had to admit that last night had been nice. He'd been so worried about Amy, wondering if his past had finally caught up with him, that he'd been unable to sleep. Claude touching him in a soothing way actually helped calm him. He'd managed to fall asleep before they even got to the good stuff. He couldn't remember the last time someone had held him...assured him everything would be okay. Hell, he couldn't remember the last time he'd truly relaxed.

Nick threw off the sheets. He sniffed the air, the scent of homemade breakfast floating into his nose. Still dressed in his T-shirt and boxers, Nick left the room. The scent grew stronger as he proceeded down the hallway that led into the kitchen, joined by the sound of clanging pots.

"Claude." Nick entered the kitchen.

Two women turned in his direction with startled expressions. The older one—a short, robust woman with gray-peppered hair worn in a bun—jumped. "Ay, *Dios mío*," she exclaimed. "You frightened me."

"Sorry. I didn't mean to."

"Please, it's all right. Señor Claude didn't mention he had an overnight guest."

Nick took a seat at the island, uncomfortable in only his underwear. "Where is Claude anyway?"

"He left already. Probably for work. I'm Vicky. This is my daughter, Yesenia." She pointed to the slightly taller, younger woman beside her.

Yesenia was beautiful and curvy, with long jet-black waves and pouty lips. She appeared around Nick's age. "We work for Señor Claude as his maids," Vicky continued.

"Oh." Nick refrained from rolling his eyes, though he was tempted to. He knew rich people were often busy, but maids? Seriously?

"Would you care for some breakfast, too?" Before Nick could say no, Vicky set a plate in front of him. There were apple cinnamon crepes with whipped cream, scrambled eggs, a fruit salad, and homemade hash browns. His stomach growled at the divine smell. Yesenia poured him a glass of orange juice.

"Thanks." While they finished cleaning, Nick scarfed down his food, emptying his entire plate in five minutes flat.

Vicky gave him a warmhearted smile. "Did you enjoy the meal?"

"Everything was delicious. Claude is a lucky guy if he gets to eat like this every day."

Vicky laughed heartily. "I said the same thing when he hired me, and he's kept me around since. Thank you for the compliment."

"Thanks for the meal." Nick left them to their work and headed for the bathroom. He'd only slept four hours, so he hoped a cold shower would revitalize him. The master bathroom was done up in white marble, chrome, and glass. Beneath the lighted vanity mirror, the countertop was veined marble with two unique sinks that were essentially large crystal bowls with steel, bamboo-style faucets. In the center of the space sat a marble Jacuzzi tub surrounded by four pillars, reminding Nick of ancient Roman or Grecian design. The earthy, spicy scent of whatever expensive cologne Claude wore lingered in the air.

Nick peeled off his underwear and slipped into the shower space. The door was frosted glass. The inside was made of limestone and marble with multiple showerheads to douse someone from different directions. Nick adjusted the dials to warm and bathed quickly. When he finished, he stepped outside and wrapped a towel around his waist. There were two walk-in closets in the bathroom. The one to Nick's left was filled to the brim with Claude's clothing. The other one was empty. That one, Claude told him to use during his stay. Nick refused. It was too permanent that way.

Nick dressed and left the bedroom. Vicky and Yesenia were gone by the time he entered the kitchen. He zipped up his coat before stepping into the elevator. Once outside, Nick exhaled a deep breath. The air there didn't smell as bad as it did back home. The streets were cleaner, the area nicer, and the noise level was tolerable. There were a lot more things to see and do, and he didn't feel so damn depressed at his immediate surroundings. However, Nick did cough a little at the overpowering smell of car exhaust, gas, and pollution.

An older man wearing an honest-to-God tuxedo stood beside him. "I'm Frances," he said in a deep European-accented voice.

Nick arched a brow at him. "Okay?"

Frances gave him a harsh stare. "I am Claude's personal driver. He said I was to take you wherever you wish to go today."

"Oh." First maids and then a personal driver? "Sure, you can drive me somewhere. As long as your car has heat, I'm good. It's freezing out here."

Frances smiled, although it didn't help soften his hard features. "Come." Frances led him to a black Bentley coupe. The car had tinted windows and was so detailed, it shone.

Nick grinned in anticipation. "That is one beautiful car." He'd liked Claude's Ferrari, but that one was more his style.

Frances opened the passenger door for him, and Nick slid inside. The interior was impressive, with its leather and modern fixtures, and roomier than he'd initially thought. It even had that new-car smell.

Nick wanted to run his fingers across the smooth dashboard and tinker around with the fancy configurations, but he balled his fists in his lap and kept them there. He didn't want Frances to shoot him or anything.

"Do you know how to get to East 114th Street?" he asked.

Frances nodded without looking at him. "Jenkins' Jazz Bar?"

Nick raised a suspicious brow. "How'd you know?"

"It's the only place in that area Claude frequents." Frances spat the words like he'd get herpes if he said them any softer. "To see you, yes?"

"Yeah." Not that he wanted Claude to. In fact, he wished Claude would stop hanging around his job. It was confusing his coworkers.

"I'll take you there."

They rode in silence. No music. No conversation. Just Frances staring straight ahead, barely blinking, and Nick staring outside the window as Fifth Avenue disappeared into the seedier, filthier hovel he resided in.

He wished he'd sat in the back.

His phone rang, breaking the uncomfortable silence. It was Eric. "I'm outside work, waiting for you. You on your way?"

Nick nodded, even though Eric couldn't see him. "Yeah, I'll be there in a few."

"All right. Hurry up, man. Fucking freezing my *cojones* off out here."

"Then go inside."

"You ain't funny, *vato*."

Nick laughed. Jenkins didn't open until the evening. "I'll be there." He hung up. "You think you could drop me off about a block from the bar?" He didn't want Eric to catch sight of him pulling up in a fancy ass Bentley. The guy would drive him crazy asking questions. He'd have no choice but to tell him about the nature of his relationship with Claude.

Frances grunted in acknowledgement. Moments later, he brought the car to a stop in front of Our Lady of Mount Carmel.

Nick hopped out. "Thanks. By the way, don't wait here for me. I'll find my own way back." Huddling against the frigid air, Nick hurried to the bar.

He spotted Eric leaning against the front door, a lit cigarette dangling from his lips. He appeared to be in a daze, his dark gaze focused on something in the distance.

Nick sidled up beside him. "Got any more of those?" he whispered into Eric's ear.

Eric jumped, eyes wide. His cigarette fell onto the ice-covered ground. Once he saw Nick, his features softened. "Don't be doing that shit, bro. I almost pulled my switchblade out on you."

Nick grinned. "Don't be spacing out in the middle of the sidewalk of fucking East Harlem. You're lucky it's daytime."

Eric shook his head as he retrieved another cigarette. "Crazy white boys, I tell you. You watch too many horror flicks."

Nick made a sound of disagreement. He didn't really go for horror, except for *The Walking Dead*. "Where were you anyway?" He pointed at Eric's bandanna-clad forehead. "Lost up here somewhere?"

"Just thinking about stuff. You ready to go see our Little Asian?"

Nick's smile softened. "Little Asian" had been his nickname for Amy due to the long dark hair she'd had. Somehow, in the last few years, Eric started calling her that, too. "Yeah, let's go."

The train ride took ninety minutes to get upstate, to the New York Med, the hospital where Amy was being treated. Nick exhaled a cold breath as he peered up at the large white-and-brown building.

"I hate the Bronx," he mumbled. If not for Amy, he'd never step foot in that borough again.

They entered the first-floor lobby. The receptionist, who was familiar with him, signed them in and got their visitation passes without delay. Nick and Eric boarded the elevator to the Inpatient Care Unit. Nick dreaded walking down those hallways, seeing all the sick people. That floor called to mind death. Not only was it cold and sterile, the space also smelled like antiseptic and metal. He hated Amy being in that place, and he made sure to make her forget about what she was going through, if only for a few hours.

Nick knocked twice on Amy's door before he pushed it open. Amy was lying in bed with a *Shojo Beat* magazine in her lap. Besides the tiredness on her pretty face, she looked happily lost in whatever manga she was reading.

"Hey, can we come in?"

Amy glanced at them, her smile widening. "Yeah! Come in." Like she often did as a little girl, she held out her arms for Nick's embrace.

Nick choked back his emotions as he hugged her, careful not to squeeze her frail body too hard. "How are you feeling today?"

"I'm great. How about you guys?"

Nick moved aside so Eric could also hug her. He plopped down on the edge of her bed. "We're good. I see you're wearing the hat I bought you." Nick nodded to the *Hamtaro* fleece beanie she'd pulled over her head. He'd gotten the hat for her for Christmas two years before.

Amy tugged at the strings. "I know, I'm getting too old for this, aren't I?"

Nick shook his head. She looked as adorable in it that day as she had then.

"I was feeling cold earlier. And I wanted to wear it, so..."

"It's cold as bricks in here," Eric said. "Whose *trasero* do I need to kick to get them to turn on some heat for my Little Asian?"

Amy laughed. "You're so funny, Eric. I'm fine now. This hat is keeping my head warm. And this book is keeping my heart warm."

Nick smiled. He was glad to hear it. "What did your doctor say?"

"That she wants me to stay a few more days so they can monitor my white blood count. Honestly, I can't wait to go home. I'm sick of being here." Amy groaned. "I miss my bed."

"I know, Aims, but you know it's important for her to monitor your blood cells. You know what happens when they get too low." Nick didn't want to consider the possibilities. Ever since Amy had been diagnosed with acute lymphoblastic leukemia, he'd been extra careful to make sure Amy stuck to the doctor's orders. He knew how much the chemo treatments and inpatient stays wore her down, and he hated it for her.

That God continued to allow her suffering was another reason why he no longer believed.

Amy nodded. "Yeah. You don't have to remind me. I'm not a baby. Besides, I'm allowed to complain every once in a while."

Eric snickered. "Oh damn. Amy's got *sass,* yo. What are you reading anyway?" He peered at the magazine.

Amy closed it shut before he got a good look. Her pale cheeks were stained red from embarrassment. "Nothing."

"What do you mean 'nothing'? It's definitely something. It's not porn, is it?"

She gaped. "Eww, no. I'm not a pervert like you, Eric."

"I'm a pervert? I'm not—"

Nick tuned out their playful banter. He stared out the window, reminiscing about the girl Amy used to be. The beautiful little girl with dark green eyes, same as his, and flowing black locks, bursting with unbelievable energy. Aside from her hair, nothing had changed, except she'd become a strong young woman. Despite everything, Amy hadn't lost the spark in her eye.

Amy's sudden coughing fit startled Nick back into the moment. "You okay?" he and Eric asked simultaneously.

Amy nodded. "Yeah, I'm just really thirsty. I'd love a pop right now."

"I'll go get it," Eric volunteered. "What kind do you drink, *hermanita?*"

"Sprite, please."

"All right. I'll be back." Eric closed the door behind him to give them some privacy.

Nick took Amy's hand in his, attempting to rub some heat back into the cold digits.

"Nick."

"Hm?"

"Mom was here earlier."

Nick froze, his gaze glued to her slender fingers.

Amy squeezed his hand. "Mom misses you, Nick. She really wants to talk to you again. You're all she thinks about."

"Don't," Nick replied in a guttural voice. He couldn't hear that. Not then. Not ever.

"She's doing so much better. Why don't you talk to her?"

"I can't." He met Amy's confused gaze, hoping she noticed the seriousness. The anger. The pain. "I won't ever talk to her again."

"Why not?" Amy snatched her grip out of Nick's. "Why do you hate her so much? What's wrong with you?"

Nick bit down on his tongue. He refused to tell Amy about his relationship with their mother. He would never burden her with that. "Calm down, Amy."

"Mom's trying! Why won't you try, too? It's your fault we can't be a family again." She clutched her chest as her coughing fit returned.

"I'm sorry." More than seeing her sick, Nick hated seeing her upset. "But I won't apologize for the rift between me and Mom. That's on her, not me. If you wanna know why so bad, I suggest you ask her."

Amy shook her head, solemnly resigned. "I have asked. Lots of times. She won't tell me anything."

Someone knocked on the door once before coming inside. "Hey, guys, it's just me." Eric handed off a bottle of Sprite to Amy with a straw. "Here you go." He handed one to Nick, also. "Everything all right?"

Nick nodded, though he didn't look away from Amy while she sipped her pop and focused on the magazine. The unshed tears in her eyes stabbed him through the gut. "Everything's good."

They didn't stay long. After an uncomfortable fifteen minutes, Amy declared she wanted to sleep.

Nick kissed her on the forehead before he left. "I'll see you soon, Aims."

She didn't respond.

They closed the door behind them.

In the hallway, Nick threw his bottle against the wall. The cap popped off and the clear fizz spilled onto the floor.

"Jesus, Nick," Eric exclaimed. "What if a couple ERs with a gurney pass through here and slip?"

Nick didn't hear him. He kept walking until he reached the elevator and pressed the down button. He needed to get the hell out of there.

Eric followed him inside the steel box. "I respect you enough not to ask, even though I noticed the shift in moods once I got back."

"Appreciate it."

"But I will ask this. What the hell happened after I left?"

Nick frowned. "What?"

"When we left work last night. That guy from the bar called you over, remember? Well, he said 'Christian,' whatever the hell that means."

Nick raked a hand through his hair. He'd forgotten all about the previous night—the break-in, moving in with Claude, the vandalized picture of Amy. His blood boiled at the thought. The desire to visit Amy, to make sure she was safe, had been overpowering that morning.

Nick noticed his friend's expectant pout. "Nothing happened."

"Nothing?"

"I mean, the guy's into me, that's all. I told him to stop following me, and then I took the bus home." Nick pushed through the glass doors, out into the cold. A woman carrying a sick child approached. The little girl ogled him.

"Mama," she said, "he's got pretty eyes."

"Yes, he does, baby."

Nick smiled softly. One thing he *actually* did miss about living in the Bronx was how friendly the people were. Despite the bad rep the media heaped on it, Nick knew the Bronx as the friendliest borough in NYC. Manhattan might be fancier, but the people were rude as hell. And so damn suspicious. Nick shoved his fists in his pockets and trekked back to the train.

Eric trudged beside him. "Is that it? Nothing else happened?"

"No. Why?"

"Don't play stupid with me, *cabrón*. I heard about the break-in."

Nick gaped at him. "How do you know?"

"Don't worry about it. My bad I missed your call, man. You gonna tell me what happened really?"

Nick carried straight ahead, observing the Italian-style row houses they passed by on the opposite side of the street, the group of outgoing friends heading into a local deli, and the bare trees Nick knew would be green and leafy in the springtime—anything to keep from having to explain last night to Eric. Even though he knew he couldn't avoid the topic forever. Eric could be a persistent bastard.

"Nick?"

"All right, Jesus," Nick said, resigned. "When I got home, pigs were there. Told me my apartment had been broken into and vandalized."

"Fuck, man. How bad was it?"

"It was bad. My place was completely trashed. Shit broken. Walls scratched up. Assholes even ransacked my refrigerator." More than that devastation, nothing hit him harder than the defiled image of his sister. That, he would never forgive. "I tried to call you."

"I know, Nick. Sorry about that. Shit."

They descended into the dimly lit train station. It wasn't as crowded as Nick expected. He and Eric made their way through the passageways, bypassing singers, chatters, beggars, and confused tourists who stood out like a sore thumb, until they got to the turnstiles leading to their platform.

They stood side by side, silent, while a young woman sang about heaven not waiting for someone.

Eric broke the silence between them. "Where'd you go last night, anyway? I hope you didn't stay at your place after what happened."

Nick stared across the tracks at the terra-cotta wall decorations. A part of him wanted to lie to Eric, but he couldn't. The truth would come out eventually. "I spent the night at Claude's."

"Claude? Mr. Upper East Side from the bar?"

Nick cringed at the bitterness in his friend's tone. "Yeah, that's him." He flashed over at Eric in time to see the irritated scowl. His jaw was rigid and his eyes were squinted. Nick's stomach dropped.

"Are you sure that's safe? I mean, you hardly know the dude."

Nick shrugged, trying to exude a confidence he didn't feel. Not when it came to Claude. The guy was too much of an enigma. "He's cool. I mean, he *did* save me from that thief last week."

"What does he want in return?"

Only for me to be his live-in lover.

"I don't know," Nick replied. "He hasn't said anything."

Eric tsked. "It's only a matter of time. Watch. Soon enough he's gonna be trying to get in them drawers."

Nick shoved at him but didn't comment. Eric didn't need to know he'd already accomplished that goal. "Don't worry so much. I can take care of myself."

Chapter Eight

CLAUDE PEEKED AT his watch. It was four o'clock. He checked the elevator door for what seemed like the hundredth time, but the thing hadn't opened.

Christian was gone.

Claude poured more whiskey into his glass and swallowed it. Frances's words filled his mind. His driver had told him he'd dropped Christian off a block away from his job. However, Jenkins' Jazz Bar didn't open until later that evening. That wasn't everything Frances told him. He'd tailed Christian, where he'd met with a friend, and they'd taken the bus together somewhere. Claude was certain that "friend" was Eric.

How suspicious.

They'd been gone together all that time. Doing what, Claude had no idea, though the possibilities were endless.

Christian hadn't even called him. Claude clenched the delicate snifter hard enough that the glass shattered. He glanced at the open cuts on his palm. The alcohol burned them. He cringed at the sight before moving to clean and bandage his hand.

"How unsightly of me," he mumbled.

Moments later, the doors slid open.

Claude perked at the sound. He composed himself before he entered the living room, not wanting to make a complete fool of himself.

Christian shoved his coat into the front closet. He nodded at Claude, who watched him from the doorway, arms folded across his sweater-clad chest.

"Hey," Christian said.

"Where were you?"

"Hospital," Christian replied in a matter-of-fact manner.

With Eric? The words settled on the tip of Claude's tongue, but he didn't ask. He already knew the answer. Hearing Christian confirm his suspicions would only upset him more. "Frances told me he dropped you off near your work. I assume you took public transportation to get there?"

"Yeah." Christian brushed past him on the way down the hallway, headed for the guest room. "Isn't that what normal people do?"

Claude followed him, confounded by Christian's blasé attitude. "Yes. Normal people who hadn't had their apartment broken into the night before."

Christian turned toward him. The expression on his face was resignation, plain and simple. Of course he couldn't deny that Claude made a good point.

Claude continued, "From now on, I would appreciate it if you allowed Frances to take you wherever you need to go, no matter how far. He won't mind. Public transportation isn't safe right now. Whoever broke into your home was obviously looking for you. They'll easily find you on one of those things." Claude closed the distance between them, placing his hands on Christian's stiff shoulders. He stared into eyes he'd missed looking into. Eyes he was elated to see again. "Will you just do as I say this time?"

"All right. Fine."

"Good." Claude placed a chaste kiss on his forehead. "Go put your coat back on. I'm taking you to dinner."

Christian scowled. "Why?"

Claude arched a brow. "What do you mean, 'why'?"

"I mean..."

Claude waited patiently while Christian racked his brain for an excuse. A slow smile spread across Claude's face. His lover was flustered. "Well?"

"I don't have anything to wear."

Claude chuckled. "Don't worry about that. Grab your coat."

Claude planned to take Christian shopping at one of his favorite department stores, Lord & Taylor. The shop was a few blocks away from his apartment, so Claude chose to walk. They strode side by side down West 38th Street, passing by a modeling agency, four-star restaurants, an artsy coffeehouse, and luxury hotels. Claude glanced at Christian. Though he appeared to be uninterested, his gaze roamed around like a cat's in new surroundings.

Christian noticed his stare. He shoved his hands into his pocket and pouted. "It smells like wet puppies out here."

Claude smiled. "It is New York City, after all. Although I will admit to preferring the smell here to urine."

Christian grinned.

Claude added, "I'm still surprised to find you living in that part of town."

Christian shrugged. "Not everyone can afford to live like you do, man."

"I've touched a sore spot. I apologize."

"No, it's cool. I know you didn't mean anything by it."

They walked together in tense silence as they neared the flagship store's gold-and-glass main entrance. Claude took a gander at the potential shoppers, every single one with the same idea as he, despite the biting cold temperature. Those who lived nearby had no qualms about walking to the luxury boutiques or various attractions. Fifth Avenuers usually didn't stray far from Fifth Avenue.

"What happened to your hand?" Christian asked, breaking the silence.

Claude's gaze lowered to the bandages. "An unfortunate accident."

They entered the store, and Claude led the way to the men's suit department. Within moments of browsing, he picked out a Hugo Boss two-piece, slim-fit wool suit. In tan, to bring out the color of Christian's eyes.

Claude called over an associate. "Bring your measuring tape."

Christian studied the price tag. "Eight hundred bucks? Are you shitting me?"

Claude tilted his head in question. "Not enough? Well, I'm sure we can find something better."

"Are you insane?" Christian shook his head. "You're really willing to drop almost a thousand dollars on some guy you barely know?"

"Don't ever say that again," Claude growled. He knew Christian better than anyone. The four years they'd spent together hadn't been for nothing. Getting to know Christian, and learning to love him despite his flaws, was the sole reason why Christian's disappearance hurt so much.

When the associate approached with the measuring tape, Claude nodded in Christian's direction. "Measure him." He wished he had a cigarette.

Christian avoided meeting Claude's gaze while the man took measurements of his neck, chest, sleeves, waist, and hips. The suit fit him perfectly.

They spent the next hour shopping, much to Christian's chagrin. It was apparent his lover didn't wish to be there. His persistence that Claude not purchase anything else for him irritated. Claude closed his eyes and counted to ten. He didn't remember Christian being so ungrateful. He used to love shopping together.

Once they finished at Lord & Taylor, Christian had an entire new wardrobe of designer sweatshirts, jeans, which Christian had insisted on, polos, casual button-down shirts, a few blazers, and dress shoes. Though Christian fought him on it, Claude had also bought him two ties, cufflinks, a new wallet, and a pair of Ray-Ban sunglasses.

Christian looked sick after seeing the amount Claude signed for. "I already told you, I'm not gonna be able to pay you back for all of this."

"I already told *you* that I don't need your money. It's a gift, so enjoy it. Please."

Christian stared at him for a long moment. He licked his lips as he grabbed several of the bags. "All right. Thank you."

Frances waited for them outside. He helped load their items into the trunk and drove them back to Claude's penthouse. "I'll bring your things up, sir," Frances said.

Claude nodded to him and led Christian inside, an arm loosely draped around his shoulders. His good mood had been restored with four words. Claude looked forward to dinner. "Why don't you shower and wear the suit tonight? I'm taking you somewhere special."

"Yeah, okay."

Claude locked up behind him. He started for the bathroom, but Christian pulled his arm. Before Claude could even frown, Christian kissed him hard. Claude's back hit the door, but Christian followed him, refusing to separate. Claude gave in to the eager young man.

He parted his lips, and Christian didn't hesitate to fill him with his tongue, tasting and exploring him. Claude's cock hardened. Christian tasted divine, not unlike an exotic prosecco. He could scarcely breathe as Christian massaged him where he ached most. As Christian reached for his belt, Claude grabbed his wrists.

"You don't have to do this." Though it would physically hurt him if Christian stopped then, he would not accept his lover thinking he had to pay such a price for anything Claude did for him.

"I know. But for some reason, I want to."

Claude chuckled. "I'm relieved to hear it." He planted a trail of balmy kisses to Christian's neck, suckling the skin to redness. His cock strained under Christian's skilled scrutiny while he undid his pants. He yearned to be buried inside him again.

Christian dropped to his knees in front of him. "Relax for me."

Claude sucked in a deep breath, staring into those lust-filled green eyes. Unable to speak, he braced himself.

Christian wet his lips. He took hold of Claude's erection and dragged his tongue along the shaft.

Claude threw his head back, moaning as pleasure hit him like thunderbolts. "God," he choked out. It'd been too long since Christian had initiated that type of intimacy with him. Claude had all but given up after Christian disappeared a year before. However, he was back home. Where he belonged.

Claude cupped Christian's cheek. He was real. "I must be dreaming," he whispered in a hoarse voice.

Christian shook his head, a soft smile on his sensuous lips. Those lips Claude wanted to drink from all night long. Christian circled the head of his penis with his tongue before he leisurely took him into his scorching mouth.

Claude ran his fingers through his hair. "Oh, Christian."

Christian focused on his task. He sucked him hard and slow, skillfully dragging his tongue in all the right places. He massaged Claude's balls.

Stars filled Claude's vision. He thrust his hips toward Christian's mouth as the pleasure built, threatening to explode like a shaken bottle of carbonated soda. "I'm coming," he warned.

Christian didn't stop. He sucked him faster, took him all the way until the tip of Claude's cock touched the back of his throat.

Claude couldn't hold back any longer. His vision flickered as he came hard in Christian's mouth.

To his surprise, Christian swallowed him up. There was no revulsion in his lusty gaze.

Claude stared at him, stunned. He well remembered how disgusted Christian had been by swallowing. He'd always demanded a warning so he could pull away right before. This time was different. Claude refused to analyze what that meant. Instead, he pulled Christian to his feet and held him tight.

"I love you," he whispered.

THEY ARRIVED AT the Georges Hotel, a French-style luxury resort in Midtown Manhattan, later that evening. Claude had reservations for two at Matteo's, a five-star Italian restaurant.

"I look okay?" Christian asked for the third time in the last half hour.

Claude noted Christian's discomfort. He fidgeted with his suit as if unused to wearing one, and smoothed his hand through his hair, keeping down imaginary flyaways.

"You look wonderful," Claude assured him.

Christian didn't say anything as they sauntered inside the atmospheric restaurant. Claude approached the maître d'. "Reservation for two. Vanderpoel."

"Right this way, sir." He led them to their own private booth on the second floor, away from the other diners. They passed by dark cherrywood tables, polished to a shine, decorated with Italian tablecloths. Each table also housed a single candle motif for intimacy. The divine scent of prepared meals and sumptuous fruits and desserts wafted to his nose. In the near distance, the soft romantic melody of a violin hummed through the restaurant.

The maître d' directed them to a booth with plush maroon seats.

Claude sat across from Christian at the candlelit table. "Nice, isn't it?"

Christian nodded, his gaze going around the dim space with its multiple candelabras, mosaics, and stained-glass windows. "I feel like we're inside an ancient church."

Their waiter approached. Claude ordered an antipasto of bruschetta for them, as well as a bottle of their finest white wine.

The waiter jotted their order and left.

Claude faced Christian. "Why were you at the hospital today?"

"I went to see my sister."

"I see. Is this the same sister you stole money from me for?"

Christian's face reddened. "Yeah," he replied gruffly, averting his gaze. "I told you she has leukemia."

Claude wasn't sure whether he believed him. As far back as he remembered, Christian had never mentioned a sister. In fact, he'd specifically told him he was an only child. Claude didn't appreciate the lies.

"I'm sorry to hear it."

"Don't worry about it."

When the waiter returned and filled their glasses, Claude noted how quickly Christian grabbed his and drank.

"What would you like to order, sir?"

Claude pointed at Christian. "You first."

"Okay. I'll have the Chianti-braised short ribs with a side of fettuccine Alfredo."

The waiter took note on his electronic pad. "Very good, sir. And for you, sir?"

"I'll have the chicken marsala with a side of rosemary potatoes."

"Thanks for taking me out," Christian said once the waiter left again. "I hope you don't mind, but I'm fucking starving."

"It's fine. Order as much as you like."

Christian dug into the platter of bruschetta. Claude didn't join him. His mind was too focused on other things. "Tell me about your sister. What's her name? How old is she?"

Christian stopped midchew and glared at him, almost suspiciously. He sipped his wine, seeming to debate whether he should answer him or not. He wondered if Christian was going over whatever lie he planned to spew.

"Amy," Christian finally replied after several moments. "She just turned sixteen."

"Still so young. How long since her diagnosis?"

"Sorry, but I don't wanna talk about this right now."

Of course he wouldn't. Claude smiled, even though he knew it didn't reach his eyes. "I understand. No reason to spoil our meal with this sort of talk."

After a tense dinner and tiramisu dessert, Frances drove them to the Empire State Building. Claude figured it'd been a while since Christian's last visit, plus the building would be illuminated in honor of Presidents' Day that night.

Christian seemed to be in a better mood as he gawked out the window in awe of their surroundings. "What's that supposed to be?"

Claude followed where Christian pointed. The strange little building neighbored alongside the skyscraper. It was actually quite ugly, with tan-colored brick and angular window boxes. However, the eastern edge extended out into a graceful curve.

"Good eye," Claude said. "It used to be Spear & Company, a furniture store built in the 1930s. The design was really high-tech modern in its time. You may not notice it, but the left side is made entirely of limestone."

"Cool."

Frances let them out, and Claude led Christian inside the renovated art-deco lobby of the Empire State Building.

"Wow. It looks like everything's made of gold in here."

Claude chuckled. "Come on." There were tourists and natives alike, enjoying the exhibits, though Claude didn't head there. He was taking Christian to the 102nd floor. They rode the manually operated Otis elevator to the Top Deck, feeling the altitudes rise with the ascent.

Christian pressed his face close to the glass, peering out at the lighted grid of streets.

Warmth spread through Claude's chest. He was glad he'd decided to bring him there.

When the doors finally opened, the cold air hit them hard, but Christian didn't seem to care. Claude didn't either. He followed behind his excited lover as he stared out at the city from up high.

"I can't believe how beautiful New York City looks from up here."

Claude couldn't agree more. The moon cast an incredible glow over the city. From their vantage point, he took in downtown, the Hudson River, rooftop pools and gardens scattered throughout Manhattan, along with other skyscrapers from almost eighty miles away.

Christian continued, "Like this, you'd never realize how much filth was actually down there."

Claude laughed softly. He wrapped his arms around Christian's waist from behind, holding him. They would be undisturbed until they finished. Claude made sure of that. "You're quite the cynic."

"I'm just a realist. I live down there. I've seen what this city can do to you."

Claude kissed his head. Realist or not, Christian could be whatever he wanted, as long as he stayed by Claude's side while he was at it.

Chapter Nine

NICK STEPPED OFF the elevator.

He threw his work apron onto his shoulder as he walked the long hallway toward Amy's hospital room. Yesterday, Claude had *insisted* he stay home so they could spend the day together. Though Nick had reluctantly agreed, he didn't have any regrets. Yesterday had been nice. He'd definitely planned to go into work the next day, though, whether Claude liked it or not.

Nick checked his watch. It was just past noon. He had a few hours to kill before his shift started.

"Hey, Nick."

Nick peered up at the smiling redheaded nurse addressing him. For the life of him, he could never remember her name. "Hey. How's it going?"

She tucked her clipboard beneath her arm. "Good. I left Amy's room a while ago. She's been a little sick, but she's doing much better."

Nick forced a smile. "Thanks."

"No problem. By the way, your mom's here today."

Nick froze, swearing after the nurse cruising down the hall toward her next patient. Blood rushed to his head, triggered by being in the same vicinity with his mother.

Nick closed his eyes. He didn't feel like deep breathing, but he did anyway. He didn't want to upset Amy.

The door to Amy's room was cracked open enough for him to peer inside. Amy was asleep, while Nicole Martin sat bedside, stroking her daughter's arm. Nick studied her profile. He didn't know whether she was lost in thought or high. Probably the latter. It wouldn't be the first time. He slipped inside.

"What the hell are you doing here?"

Nicole jumped in her chair, placing a hand over her heart. Her startled expression relaxed once she realized who'd spoken. "Jesus, Nick. You scared the crap out of me." She hesitantly got to her feet, as if he was some sort of holy figure, and studied him.

Nick studied her, too. She'd lost weight since the last time he'd seen her. She looked tired, and her bleached-blonde hair needed a root touch-up in the worst way. Her pink sweater and blue jeans hung loosely off her petite frame. Regardless, that was his mother. Like it or not. She might look wizened, but Amy's resemblance to her was uncanny.

Nicole broke the silence first. "So, how have you been? You look well."

"I'm fine."

Nicole cleared her throat. "Dr. Thompson told me that Amy's been sick all day. She gave her something to help her sleep."

"That's good." He walked to the bed to check on his little sister. Her chest rose and fell as she breathed slowly but steadily, in a deep sleep.

Longing filled Nicole's pale face as she studied his movements like a hawk. Her eyes glossed over with unshed tears.

Nick grew taut as she approached, a hand outstretched to touch him. "Don't."

Nicole froze before she made contact. She searched his features for something—any sign of affection.

Nick didn't give in to her. She'd had her chance long ago to be his mother.

"I miss you, Nick. That's the reason why I'm here. I wanted to see Amy, but I also hoped to talk to you."

"We have nothing to talk about," Nick snapped.

The dam broke. Tears spilled down her cheeks. Nick didn't care. Or at least, he told himself he didn't. He'd always hated to see her cry, though. Jesse had made her cry all the time, and he'd wanted to strangle the man for it.

"I just... I just want to apologize," Nicole said, "for not believing you." She hugged her own trembling body tight, her eyes haunted. "What kind of mother doesn't believe her own child when he tells her something like that?"

Nick closed his eyes, assaulted with memories. Memories of his own mother slapping him and calling him a liar when he'd come to her for help.

Nicole continued, "I think somehow I'd always known."

"Of course you did," Nick said in a low voice. "You didn't *want* to know, but you knew. You knew where he went all those late nights. Knew he was creeping into my room." Nick swallowed hard. "You knew he was touching me."

She seemed pained by his words, her eyes red and brimming with more tears. "I know I can't change the past, Nick. I know I have no right to ask for your forgiveness. But please, if there's anything I can do to make things right between us, I'll do it."

Nick straightened. There was one thing. "Make me Amy's legal guardian."

Nicole shook her head. "You know I can't do that."

"Why not?"

"Because Amy is all I have left." She slapped her hands against her sides in defeat. She had to realize their relationship could never be salvaged.

"What happened to Jesse?" Nick asked.

"He's in jail."

Nick gaped. "Jail?" He'd had no idea. Not that he involved himself in family affairs anymore...

Nicole nodded. "About six months ago, they threw him in jail for rape. It's just been me alone, trying to get back on my feet and be a better mother to her. And to you."

Nick schooled his features into stoicism. He didn't need a mother. Not anymore. "I sympathize, but I won't let you fail Amy like you did me."

She looked as if he'd slapped her. Nick averted his gaze so he wouldn't have to see the hurt. He knew he was being too harsh, but he also felt justified in his anger.

"I understand." Nicole reached for her purse near Amy's bed. She clutched the leather bag to her like a lifeline while she backed into the door. "When she wakes, will you please tell her I was here? And that I love her?"

"Yeah," Nick choked out.

"I know you don't believe me. I know you hate me, but I love you too, Nick. And I'm trying. I really am." She left the room before he could say anything.

Nick took her seat at Amy's bedside. He gripped a filled Styrofoam cup and crushed it. Water spilled onto his hand and dripped on his jeans, but he didn't care. His temples throbbed. That was why he hadn't wanted her there in the first place.

"I need a drink," Nick said aloud. He skimmed over Amy's sleeping profile, then got up and left the room. He intended on getting a few pops and coming back before she woke up to be dragged off somewhere.

Nick pulled open the door and froze. Claude stood in front of him, his right fist poised to knock. "What are you doing here?"

Claude lowered his hand. He smiled softly at Nick. "I followed you."

"What?"

"I wanted to see for myself if there was any truth to what you told me at dinner the other night. About having an ill younger sister. It seems you weren't lying, after all."

Nick's nostrils flared with fury at Claude's nonchalant attitude. As if trailing someone was the most normal thing in the world.

"Was that your mother who just left?" Claude pointed in the direction Nicole must have gone.

"Yes," Nick answered through clenched teeth.

"Can I meet her?"

"Who? My mother?"

"No." Claude pointed at Amy, still sleeping in bed. "Your sister. I'd like to meet her."

Nick's eyes darkened. "Stay the hell away from her."

Chapter Ten

CHRISTIAN IS GONE forever and it's my fault.

Claude woke with a startled gasp. His skin was clammy with sweat, despite the cool temperature. He glimpsed around his room, trying to make sense of his surroundings. To ground himself in reality. He scrubbed his face with trembling hands.

"It was only a dream," he assured himself.

Christian was not really gone. In fact, he lay soundly beside him.

Claude reached for the opposite side of the bed, where Christian usually slept. He received a handful of rumpled sheets and pillows. Claude's eyes widened. "Christian," he called. His dream came back to haunt him, taunting him with the possibility of losing his lover again. Claude tossed the sheet aside and hopped out of bed. He didn't care about his nakedness as he trampled across the floor to check the master bathroom. "Christian," he called again. There was no sign of him there.

Claude wandered throughout his apartment, calling Christian's name, growing more desperate. The scent of food floated into his nose. Claude ran to the kitchen. Vicky and Yesenia might be there. So might Christian. Claude pulled to a stop before he reached the space.

Christian stood in front of the stove in his pajamas, spatula in hand, earphones in his ears, singing along to whatever music he listened to. He didn't notice Claude's presence.

Claude sagged with relief, his tense shoulders going lax at the sight of him. He was still there. He hadn't left him again. Claude approached the younger male and wrapped his arms around him tightly. Christian tensed just the slightest at his touch, but Claude didn't dare let go.

"You're here," he whispered.

Christian covered Claude's hand with his own. "I apologize for yesterday. I didn't mean to go off on you like that."

"There's no need to apologize. You were upset." Besides, his presence there that morning was all the apology Claude needed.

"Okay, then. I made breakfast."

Claude glanced over his shoulder at the food on the stove, hiding his surprise. Honestly, he couldn't ever remember Christian showing any culinary inclinations. Everything looked perfect, even.

"I'm speechless."

Christian snorted. "I can cook if I need to. I've had to be self-sufficient for a long time."

"I see."

"Why don't you sit down? Or maybe you'd like to put some clothes on first?"

Claude peered down at himself. He wasn't abashed by nudity, though the circumstances surrounding his current state were a bit embarrassing. "I suppose I should."

"Don't worry. Breakfast will be done before you come back."

Claude left to quickly dress in a pair of the few sweatpants he owned. He put on a T-shirt and returned to the kitchen. True enough, Christian had set a filled plate on the island for him. There were seasoned omelets, crisp applewood bacon, and buttered toast. Christian handed him a cup of black coffee—just the way he preferred.

Claude took a seat. "Why don't you tell me about yesterday? What happened?"

Christian poured orange juice for himself and joined him. Quietly, he ate his food, his gaze straight ahead as if pondering how much—if any— he should tell Claude about what had transpired. Several moments ticked by before he finally relented.

"It's my mom," he said. "She was at the hospital yesterday. I didn't want to see her."

Claude recalled the older blonde who'd run from the room, her eyes red with tears. She'd brushed by him without ever noticing him standing there. "Why not?"

"Because I hate her."

Claude shoved a piece of omelet into his mouth. He thought of his own father, whom he did not ever get along with. However, he wouldn't go so far as to say he hated him. Even if he thought he did at times.

Christian continued, "She was never much of a mother to me growing up, but now that I'm an adult, she's trying to play that role. To make herself feel good. Well, fuck that. I don't plan on giving her the satisfaction."

"That's a bit harsh, don't you think? Especially since she's your mother. You only have one, you know."

"Spare me the bullshit lecture." Christian stabbed at his plate with his fork. "I don't need her. Never have. In fact, if I could take Amy away from her, somewhere far away where she would never find us, I'd gladly do it."

Claude sipped from his steaming mug without a word. Whatever happened between them was none of his business. Familial matters were not his forte. Besides, he'd always known Christian to be a troubled young man from the first moment he'd caught him shoplifting. Still, he wanted to take his mind off the toxic thoughts.

"Do you have work today?"

"Not until this evening. Why?"

"I have a yacht docked on the Hudson. How would you like to go for a ride?"

Christian bit his lower lip with indecision. "I don't know. Don't you think it's too cold for a boat ride?"

"Not at all. In fact, the weather's supposed to be nicer today." Claude arched a brow, genuinely confused by his lover's unwillingness. Christian never turned down the opportunity for luxury pursuits. And there were few things more luxurious than cruising on a multimillion-dollar yacht. "Unless you made other plans," Claude deadpanned, his mind filled with images of the Puerto Rican bartender, a man Christian claimed was only a friend, though Claude wondered if he could be much more.

Christian scanned him as if he knew the nature of his thoughts. "No, so yeah...I'll go with you after breakfast."

"Then eat up."

GETTING TO THE Hudson River was a two-hour drive going north on I-87. That day was unseasonably warm for February in New York, so they'd dressed moderately light for the occasion. From the back seat of the car, Claude pointed out his sixty-one-foot yacht, boasting a sleek hull design. Although Christian had been reluctant to come earlier, his exuberance proved he was glad to have changed his mind.

"What's that say on the side?" Christian asked.

"*Vrijheid*. It means 'freedom' in Dutch."

Christian repeated the word aloud. "I like that."

Several minutes later, they boarded his motor yacht, and Claude gave him a tour. He showed him the light and airy salon, with its muted neutral colors that created a simplistic, elegant atmosphere, complete with an L-shaped sofa, love seat, and full entertainment system. Wide sliding-glass doors opened to an aft deck and shaded alfresco dining option. Forward of the salon was a formal dining table on the port side with the galley on starboard. The entire space was flanked by panoramic windows allowing ample natural light and uninterrupted views.

"How fast can she go?"

"Up to thirty-six knots, but I like to cruise around twenty-five." Claude led him through the many outdoor areas, including the deck, sun pads, swim platform, and bow. Although Christian fought to contain his enthusiasm, his beaming countenance told otherwise. Claude took him to the flybridge, where his captain, Lee, waited for his direction. The flybridge was well-equipped, with double sun pads, alfresco dining, barbecue, and a collapsible cover. He directed Christian to the U-shaped sofa. "Have a seat."

Christian complied, glancing out at the navy blue waters and what few seagulls flew above their heads, their caws deafening.

Claude left to retrieve a bottle of Beringer white zinfandel. The wine tasted a bit sweet, but he had a feeling Christian might enjoy it.

Lee started the engine. Claude had relayed directions to him already. They were to cruise down the Hudson while enjoying the landmarks and scenic views of the Manhattan skyline. It would give them ample time to talk. Claude planned on finding out where Christian had gone twelve months prior.

As his yacht headed downstream, Claude returned and filled their stems. He sat beside him on the sofa. "Cheers."

Christian clinked his glass against his. "I forgot to ask, but what do you do exactly?"

"I'm the COO of a luxury boating company. You know the one my father owns." Vanderpoel Boating Industries was to be his someday, but Claude wasn't sure he wanted the responsibility. Augustus's attempts at "grooming" him to take over his business had been feverish most of his adolescent life. At the moment, they bordered on desperate. The old man was preparing to retire and sail the world with Amelia, Claude's mother. Before he left, however, he would make sure Claude was capable of handling the company himself. That included checking up on his work and being an utter nuisance.

"Sounds like you don't like your job."

"On the contrary, I do like my job. It just would not have been my first choice."

"What would have been your first choice?" Christian sipped his wine.

"I studied Economics and Marketing at Yale. I pored over the stock market for several years, so I think I would have enjoyed working on Wall Street. Either that, or becoming a university professor in Paris." He'd spent an entire semester in the city and had fallen in love with it.

"Cool."

Claude eyed the younger male. "What about you? What have you done for money in the last year or so?"

Christian scratched his head. "Not much. Working at Jenkins's bar. I've been there for a while, actually."

If only he'd found him sooner...

Claude cleared his throat. "Do you like it?"

"Yeah, I do. I mean, the money could be better, but it's decent. My coworkers are cool."

Claude could relate. He despised working with people he couldn't get along with. Since he'd become boss, however, he didn't hesitate to fire those he didn't mesh well with.

"Any new hobbies?" Claude brought his glass to his lips.

"None. I'm just trying to keep my hands clean, if you know what I mean."

Claude thought back to the thug chasing Christian outside of his workplace. He wanted badly to ask him about that, but didn't care to ruin the moment. It was neither the time nor place.

Instead, he sank back against the sofa as ferries and sailboats cruised by, their patrons obviously taking advantage of the nicer weather. The soothing sound of the melting ice floes sloshing against his yacht and the quiet roar of its two 900-horsepower engines lulled him.

Christian positioned himself close to the edge and gazed at their surroundings. "It's so surreal. I wish Amy could see this."

"She could. I'd love to bring her out here with us."

Christian didn't respond.

Neither did Claude. He excused himself and headed to the galley to instruct the chef what to prepare for lunch in a few short hours. Though in the mood for seafood, Claude settled for something with chicken. Quesadillas. After relaying instructions, Claude returned to his companion.

Christian's sharp curse startled him.

"What's wrong?"

Christian turned to him, ecstatic. "It's the Statue of frickin' Liberty, Claude! I've never been this close to it before. I feel like I can reach out and touch it. Holy hell, it's huge, too!"

Claude observed him with a keen smile. Like that, Christian resembled an exuberant child, arms outstretched, cheeks reddened from the cold wind, green orbs lit up like fire. Claude leaned in and nuzzled his cheek. Christian smelled heavenly, like Claude's soap, cologne, and home.

"Why don't you take a picture?"

Christian didn't hesitate to take out his camera phone and snap photos of the torch-bearing copper woman.

"Did you know that the Statue of Liberty was actually a gift to the United States from the French?"

"Nope." He continued to take pictures, not just of the statue, but of the skyline, the yacht, and the water.

Claude continued, "Not only does she represent the end of slavery, she's also a symbol of the strong unity between the two countries."

"Thanks for the history lesson, professor." Christian grinned.

Claude couldn't help one, as well. Christian's smile was infectious. "Why don't you take one of us?"

"What? You mean a selfie?"

Claude nodded. He wrapped an arm around Christian's waist, pulling him flush against his side. Christian frowned a little but held the camera phone up anyway. Before he snapped the picture, Claude captured his lips in a passionate kiss.

The phone slipped from Christian's grasp and fell onto the deck. "Claude," he mumbled.

"Leave it," Claude growled. "I want you. Right now."

Christian stared at him, taken aback. His eyelids lowered slightly, and he bit his lip. "Okay, yeah."

They escaped below deck where Claude took him into the master cabin.

"Man, this is really nice," Christian commented. He took in the neutral décor, with its elegant furnishings and en-suite facilities. Thanks to the sleek hull windows on both sides, the room had plenty of light and fantastic views.

Claude sat on the queen-size bed, unbuttoning his shirt. His gaze never wavered from Christian, who seemed a bit awkward, standing in one spot. Claude smiled. "It's warmer down here. Take off your jacket."

Christian obeyed without hesitation. He shrugged off the sports jacket and tossed it onto the love seat.

Claude slid off his shirt, revealing his bare chest and defined abs for his lover's viewing pleasure. "Come here."

Christian ambled toward him, his lusty expression conveying Claude's own emotion in that moment.

Claude pulled Christian to stand before him. He thrust his hand beneath Christian's shirt, touching his flushed skin. He was smooth and hard and beautiful, like an ancient marble statue. Claude burrowed his face against his abs.

"Just like David," he whispered reverentially. He reached for the button of Christian's jeans, but Christian shoved him back against the bed.

Between one breath and the next, Christian straddled his thighs, shoving his mouth onto his, consuming him.

Claude parted his lips so that his lover might explore him further. His mouth was sweet and hot, tasting of grapes and mint. Claude caressed his warm skin, every inch he could reach in their position. His heart softened at the quiet moans his lover made in reaction to his touch.

Christian pulled away first. His cheeks were flushed, his lips moist, and eyes as glassy as obsidian. "Got a condom?"

"Check the bathroom." As Christian ventured off to retrieve one, Claude pulled off his shoes and pants, though he left his briefs on. He hoped Christian would remove them, much like he'd done after their shopping excursion.

Claude listened to Christian rummage around for what seemed like forever. Finally, he exited the bathroom, disappointment etched into his features. "I don't see any."

Claude shook his head. He hadn't taken any lovers after Christian left, so there'd been no one to enjoy his yacht with. Hannah had cruised with him once or twice, but their relationship was strictly platonic and mostly professional. "I'm sorry. Next time, I'll be better prepared."

Christian straightened his straining erection in his jeans. "It's cool. We could still kiss. If you want to."

Claude's gaze darkened. Of course he wanted to. More than anything. He reached toward Christian, beckoning him. The bed made the slightest creak when Christian crawled onto it. Their lips met naturally, the feverish desperation from earlier replaced with slow, tender motions. Claude's eyes fluttered closed as he savored his lover's sweet taste.

Being able to hold him again, to feel him, was the single greatest gift.

"Turn around," Claude commanded in a husky voice.

Christian obeyed.

Claude pulled the younger male in front of him, his back pressed to Claude's hard chest. Claude's cock rested on the small of his back.

A small moan escaped Christian.

Claude smiled. He grabbed the hem of Christian's shirt and lifted the fabric above his head, needing to explore him skin to skin. He was scorching, his naturally tanned skin rosy. His chest expanded with every deep inhalation. Claude reached for his jeans once more. Heat emanated from the area, almost hot enough to singe. He went for the zipper anyway.

Christian arched into him as Claude slipped a hand inside, taking hold of his hard girth. "Jesus."

Claude whispered against his ear, "Jesus can't save you from me." He locked his mouth onto Christian's throat, lips sucking his salty goose-bump-riddled skin while stroking his pulsing flesh and massaging his heavy balls. His own cock jerked in excitement at the sensuous moans Christian elicited. His body begged for release, but he could ignore it for the moment. Claude was content to make sure of Christian's satisfaction.

"Oh, fuck, Claude." Christian threw his head back against his shoulder, his mouth open wide to suck in oxygen, it seemed. His hips gyrated with each stroke.

Claude groaned in agonized pleasure. Each time Christian rolled into him, he brushed against his weeping cock. Claude's briefs were stained with precum.

"A little harder," Christian demanded, his voice tight.

Claude happily obliged. He tightened his grip, nearly constricting, and slid up and down Christian's shaft with more difficulty.

Christian stiffened. "Fuck yeah, ah, I'm…I'm—" Semen spurted from him, coating Claude's hand. He shuddered and sank into Claude. A breathy laugh escaped him as he touched the crotch of his jeans, wet with ejaculate. "Guess I can't wear these anymore."

"I'll buy you another pair." Claude held him tightly and rained kisses onto his skin. Though his cock ached and throbbed, he would take care of that later. Nothing was going to pry him away from Christian like this. Not even his own needs.

"Promise you won't ever leave me." Claude spoke in a low voice. He was afraid Christian might hear the trembling in it.

Christian caressed Claude's bare leg, sending a tingle up the limb. "I'm not going anywhere."

Chapter Eleven

NICK TOOK A deep breath. He'd been trying to wipe the stupid smile off his face ever since he and Claude made it back to that side of town. Nick almost succeeded too, until Claude showed him how he'd reached his limit once they got back to the penthouse.

He fucked Nick with a desperation that would've been frightening if Nick hadn't been on cloud nine. His ass was sore, but Jesus, he felt like he could fly.

Nick schooled his features as best as he could before he strode inside the bar. Toasty, fried chicken-scented air and slow jazz greeted him.

His boss, Phil Jenkins, sat on the stage, playing his saxophone like no one was watching.

Nick headed for the back to clock in. It was thirty minutes past five, so the bar wasn't open to any customers yet. The cooks prepped food while the other servers gossiped and prepared extra silverware for the tables.

"Hey, Nick." Mercedes approached him with another girl in tow. Both wore big Cheshire grins.

"What's up?"

"Nothing. Just wondering what you in a good mood about."

Nick hid the grin threatening to spill. "I don't know what you're talking about."

"Mm-hm. Sure you don't. Every other day, you come to work all brooding and pissed off, but *today,* I saw a real smile."

"Still, don't know what you're talking about, Mercedes." Nick clocked in and hung up his coat and hat in the office. The two girls followed him.

"You glowing, boy!" Mercedes nudged him in the side. "Is it a girl? You cheating on me, Nick?"

Nick rolled his eyes and allowed himself to chuckle at her antics. Mercedes was only two years older than Amy. Even if he didn't prefer men, he'd never go there with her. "You two better get going before I tell Phil you're slacking off again."

The girls walked off with a giggle.

"Yo."

Nick spun around, his apron falling from his shoulder. Eric stood behind him. The lingering scent of tobacco drifted from his clothes. He must have been out back having a smoke.

"Oh hey, man. What's up?" Nick grabbed his apron and tied it around his waist.

"Someone's in a good mood."

"Oh yeah?" Nick grinned. "How could you tell?" He moved to the front to notify the host which tables he would take.

Eric followed him. "*Que onda maje?* How was your day?"

"It was cool. How was yours?"

"Probably not as good as yours. I had to do some wrangling today. Put some people in check. Family stuff. What about you?"

Nick paused to glance at him. Eric folded his muscled arms across his thick chest, an expectant look on his face. Waiting for Nick to spill his secrets or something. "What do you want me to say, E?"

Eric shrugged. "I just asked how your day was, man. Don't read too much into it."

"It was great. Fucking wonderful." He smiled at the thought of earlier. "Claude took me out on his yacht. We sailed down the Hudson and saw the Statue of Liberty. That's about it."

Eric's jaw tightened. The same angry expression he'd worn at the train station the other day. "That's it? That can't be it, bro. Did you fuck him?"

Nick's fists curled at his side, his own ire boiling. "None of your fucking business."

"Relax, dude." Eric held his hands up in a pose of surrender. He gave Nick a sly smile. "You know I don't care if you are or not. Like you said, ain't none of my business."

Nick turned away from his friend and tried to focus on his job. Serious or not, he didn't appreciate where the conversation was going.

"I'm guessing you won't have time for anyone anymore now that you're some rich guy's plaything."

IT WAS PAST two in the morning when Nick finished work. Frances waited outside to take him home.

"Hey," Nick mumbled.

Frances pulled open the passenger door without response.

Nick climbed inside. He didn't speak the entire drive back to Claude's penthouse. Didn't pay attention to any of the sights, either. Eric's words clouded his mind. They bothered him more than they should. Nick wiped at his dry eyes, trying not to remember the life he'd left behind and the memories Eric's words brought up for him.

When he entered the penthouse, Claude greeted him with a glass of white wine. "It's Montrachet." He placed a chaste kiss to Nick's lips.

"Thanks." Nick shuffled inside. The place was spotless as usual and slightly warmed from the fireplace. The scent of tomatoes, lemon, and balsamic herbs lingered in the air.

"Come into the kitchen for dinner," Claude said.

Nick remained glued to the spot. For some reason, he couldn't make himself move.

Claude frowned. "What's wrong?"

"You don't think we're moving too fast?"

"What makes you say that?"

"It hasn't even been two weeks yet, and I'm already living with you like we're a couple. I mean, we barely know each other." Nick compressed his lips into a thin line as frustration welled through him. "And why the hell are you going out of your way to help me anyway? I don't get it."

Claude sighed with exasperation. "Christian—"

"Why do you keep calling me that?" Nick interrupted. "My name's Nick. I've never been Christian."

Claude stared at him a moment, the expression in his hazel eyes filled with uncertainty and sadness. He set the glass on the table and closed the distance between them, placing his hands on Nick's shoulders.

"The reason why I go out of my way to help you is because I love you."

Nick shook his head, refusing to believe that. "How can you love me when you don't even know me?"

"I know you plenty." Claude traced a finger along his lips. "I know I was lost without you. I know I need you more than anything. You think I'm helping you, but you're the one really helping me." Claude pulled Nick into a tight embrace.

Surrounded by Claude's strong arms and the exotic spice of his cologne and Turkish tobacco, Nick's heart rate intensified, so much so, he feared Claude might hear the pounding in his chest. As all of his earlier doubts faded away, a foreign feeling flowed through him. Warmth. He felt safe in Claude's arms. Safer than he'd ever been his entire life with his parents.

"You gave me my life back," Claude whispered.

Nick gradually wrapped his arms around Claude's broad back. "You—" The wineglass slipped from his grasp and shattered against the marble floor. Nick peered down at the mess. "Sorry. I'll clean it up."

Claude squeezed him tighter, almost as if afraid to let go. "Don't worry about it."

Chapter Twelve

CLAUDE WOKE UP Saturday morning, filled with elation. He had quite the itinerary planned for Christian that day. First, they would visit the Metropolitan Museum of Art, one of Claude's personal favorites, then do some shopping on Fifth Avenue before having lunch at the Union Square Café. Afterward, perhaps a stroll through Central Park. The weather wasn't terribly cold, and he looked forward to spending more time catching up.

Claude wasn't sure what Christian had gone through in these past twelve months, but he knew his lover was a changed man. He even went by a different name these days. "Nick," Claude said aloud as he dressed in front of the bathroom mirror. Claude shook his head. He didn't like it. He would always be Christian to him.

Clearing his mind of the thought, Claude resumed his mental preparations for that day. Once they left Central Park, they would catch a Broadway show before returning to Claude's apartment for a home-cooked meal.

Christian had a day off from work, so he'd gone to visit his sister in the hospital. However, he wouldn't stay long, his words verbatim. He'd also gone alone, another thing to be relieved about.

Claude grabbed his keys and left. With nothing else to do until Christian returned, he decided to check in at the office and put that incredible energy to good use.

Hannah greeted him with a smile when he came through the door. "Good morning, sir." She dressed impeccably as usual in a red form-fitting designer pantsuit and stilettos. Her blonde locks were pulled back into a sleek ponytail, and her makeup was minimal, at best, aside from the fire-engine red painting her lips. "Care for some coffee?"

"No, I won't be staying long. I have a date, actually."

"Oh?" She tilted her head to the side curiously. "With?"

Claude beamed. Though Hannah was his employee, at times she functioned as his friend and confidante. Things he wouldn't dare breathe a word about to anyone else, he had no qualms telling her. She knew all about Christian and the torrid relationship they'd shared.

"Do you remember Christian?"

"The one who disappeared?"

Claude nodded. "He's returned." He couldn't help the broad smile spilling across his face at the thought. Christian was there to stay this time.

Hannah filled her coffee cup with creamer, appearing hesitant. "Has he?"

"I found him working in East Harlem, actually. He's living with me now."

"No wonder you've been in a good mood lately. What do you two have planned?"

Claude led the way toward his office. Hannah followed at his side, her heels clacking on the expensive tile. "The museum. Shopping. I plan to expand his new wardrobe and get rid of the god-awful clothing he's been wearing."

"Has it gotten that bad? What has he been doing in East Harlem all this time? I can't imagine him choosing to live there."

A red haze clouded Claude's vision as he remembered the first night he'd come across Christian at the bar. He'd been working for minimum wage more than likely, desperate to pay his sister's medical bills. He'd even resorted to stealing from Claude rather than ask for the money. Maybe he'd been ashamed to ask. Claude cringed at the memory of Christian's horrible living conditions. Someone had caused him to live life like that. Claude was certain it wasn't only the thug who'd chased after him. Ever since then, Christian checked over his shoulder, most of the time subconsciously. There were things he hadn't explained to Claude, either. For one, the person threatening him.

"I intend to find that out as well."

Hannah nodded, concern etching her features. "I almost forgot. Your father is waiting in your office."

Claude froze with his hand on the door handle. "How long has he been here?"

"He arrived several minutes ago."

"Thank you, Hannah. Is there anything else?"

"No, sir."

Claude schooled his features before entering his office. It would not be a pleasant visit.

Augustus reclined in Claude's seat, his dark-gray gaze skimming through files Claude kept locked away in his filing cabinet.

Physically speaking, Augustus Vanderpoel wasn't an imposing man. Not like when Claude was much younger and forced to crane his neck to the sky to look upon the man's stern face. As the years flew by and Claude grew taller and stronger, he wondered what he was ever afraid of in the first place. But then, he knew the answer to that question. His father's size hadn't been what intimidated Claude all those years back.

"Father."

Augustus didn't bother to look up. "Sit down."

Claude took a seat across from him in one of the comfortable chairs he'd arranged for visits with clients. He automatically straightened his posture in his father's presence, remembering well how much Augustus hated for him to slouch. The cloying scent of citrus, bergamot, sandalwood, and leather lingered between them. Aramis Classic, his father's favorite cologne. In another situation, Claude would say the fragrance conjured images of dimly lit gentleman's clubs or the evocative aroma of cigars, but the smell only reminded him of the childhood he'd endured with that man.

After several minutes leafing through pages, Augustus finally laced his manicured fingers on top of the black glass desk. He stared at Claude, his expression stern and unchanging. "How goes running the company? You're not having any difficulties in my absence, are you?" His voice was cultured, still holding traces of a Dutch accent, though he'd spent most of his life in the States.

"All is well," Claude replied. "The business is running smoothly."

"Is it?"

"It is."

Augustus slid over the files he'd been reading. "I've been looking through the numbers for this quarter and last, and I've found a discrepancy. Why don't you open the folder, son."

Claude hesitated before he complied. The first slip of paper on top displayed the numbers for each consecutive quarter. He quickly scanned through it, unable to spot what his father had. Claude leafed through the papers once more, then closed the file. He was tired of this game. Tired of his father's displeasure with him. If the man wanted him to know what was wrong, he could tell him.

"I don't see a problem."

Augustus snorted. "I'm not surprised you wouldn't. See here. These numbers are too low. Compare them to how high they were ten years ago. That's quite an unexpected drop."

Claude didn't flinch as he faced off with the old man. No one could predict the trend in the boating market. He'd had to adapt many times within the last few years. Not to mention, the technological advances made in the last decade alone meant more demands for the most high-tech watercraft today. Creating these boats was taking longer each year. He didn't voice that to his father. It would upset him to hear his only son "complaining" about a business that had been essentially handed to him. Instead, Claude composed himself.

"No worries. I expect the numbers to spike soon. The current trend is vacation yachts in the place of villas. We've been getting many international calls lately. Our winter is their summer in most cases."

A flash of pleasure crossed Augustus's face briefly. "I admire your tenacity with keeping up with the demands of today's market, but it's not enough. The numbers should be higher. There is no excuse for that. How will your mother and I leave when I have doubts about your ability to handle this company on your own?"

Claude folded his own hands across his lap, the desire to light a cigarette strong. It didn't matter, really. None of it did. His father would never acknowledge him, even though he worked six days most weeks, staying on top of things, studying the market, micromanaging every small detail. His adaptability and progress were usually noted by longtime clients and investors, men and women who'd established a good rapport with his father during his tenure. As uncertain as he'd been in the beginning, Claude had learned to take pride in the excellent job he was doing. Their words were the only affirmation he needed. He'd accepted that Augustus would never praise him for anything, and his stance was to be tough about everything.

"If you had doubts about my capability, then perhaps you should have left your company in the hands of your men."

Augustus's lip curled. "Don't you dare talk back to me. I'll not have any of your sass."

Claude bowed his head. "Forgive me, Father. I have much work to attend to. Do you require anything else?"

"I do, actually. It's the real reason why I'm here."

Claude waited in anticipation.

"I need you to meet with Dr. Holcomb in Providence, immediately."

Claude arched a brow. "Dr. Holcomb? He's going away on an expeditionary trip to the Amazon, correct?" Claude remembered the man as a longtime client and friend of his father's. He was also a famed archaeologist constantly going on quests around the world. "Hannah scheduled an appointment with him next month."

"I need you to meet with him today. Right now. His trip to the Amazon is happening sooner than expected. I already called the pilot to be at the airfield. If you take the company jet, you'll be in Providence in an hour."

Claude frowned, calculating the time frame in his head. The meeting with Dr. Holcomb should take no more than two hours. It was a formality, mostly, to determine the gist of what he wanted. Everything else would be done by email. Two hours wasn't bad, though factoring in the additional two hours to get back and forth, he would be gone four, possibly five hours. He'd be unable to spend the day with Christian as planned.

His annoyance must have shown because Augustus smirked. "What's the matter, son? Is this too short notice for you? Dr. Holcomb is a top client. It is in our best interest to be as accommodating as possible."

"I agree."

"Good. I'm glad we've reached an understanding. The client always comes first. That's how we've managed as top tier in this industry." Augustus rose from his seat, straightening his suit as he approached the door.

Claude stood as well to escort him out.

"I'll be visiting again soon."

Not too soon, I hope.

Augustus continued, "I expect to hear the meeting went as planned when I speak with Dr. Holcomb tonight."

Claude clenched his teeth. "Of course."

No exchanges of endearments or frivolities happened. Augustus merely nodded and left the office.

Claude released a long-held breath. That was precisely why he avoided his father. The man was a bane to his livelihood. Claude reached for his cell phone, intending to call Christian with the news. They might not get the entire day together, however they'd have time for a musical and dinner, at least. Claude dialed his number and waited while it rang.

"The person you are trying to reach is not available. At the tone, please leave a message." Beep.

"Impossible." He dialed again and waited, his jaw firm. After three rings, Christian still hadn't answered. Claude stared at the phone, at Christian's number. Thoughts filled his head. Images that made him damned-near murderous. Christian wasn't alone. He was with someone for sure. And Claude could do nothing about it.

Chapter Thirteen

NICK CRACKED OPEN his tired eyes with a wince. His temples throbbed. His throat was as dry as a desert. He glanced around, but the room was dark and quiet. He couldn't see a thing. The hair on his nape bristled.

Where the hell was he?

Nick lifted his body off the plush fabric. The darkened room swam as nausea consumed him. Bile filled his throat, threatening to spill. Nick clamped a hand over his mouth, forcing down the urge to vomit. He put his feet on the cold hardwood floor. Was he in someone's house? He racked his brain for clues, but his head only pounded more.

Guardedly, he rose to his feet, hands stretched out, trying to make sense of his surroundings. He had no idea what occupied the space with him. He just hoped he didn't kill himself attempting to find a light switch or door.

Nick's knee made contact with something hard and solid. Wood. He tumbled over the thing and fell onto his back, sending an entire array of lightweight boxes falling on top of him.

"Fuck."

A light switch came on. Someone was in the room with him.

Panicking, Nick grabbed the closest thing within reach. A video game case. Saints Row the Third. Nick eyed it with confusion.

"Jesus, Nick."

Nick peered up at the familiar voice. Eric filled the doorway, staring at him with amusement dancing in his dark gaze.

"Eric?" Nick croaked. He inspected the pile he was buried in. Somehow, he'd upended the wooden table, sending a bunch of DVDs and video games crashing onto him.

Eric's sudden clapping brought back his attention. "Good job, son."

Nick rubbed at his head, suddenly filled with embarrassment. "How did I get here?"

"You don't remember?" Eric approached him. He smelled like the pungent, earthy stench of marijuana. Eric knelt down to pick up the cases.

Nick helped him. "Nope."

"You were pretty pissed off, yo. Seeing Amy like that. We went to the bar, had us some drinks. You got wasted so I brought you to my crib. You've been sleeping like a baby since."

Nick's gaze flashed around the understated living room where he'd been sleeping, on the tan sofa. Eric had taken off his shoes and tossed his coat onto the couch. It'd been so long since Nick's last visit. The day's memories came back to him. Visiting Amy in the hospital earlier. Seeing her pale and weak, though she'd fought to ignore the pain and be in a good mood.

He'd hated watching Amy suffer.

Eric had come to check on her, too, and they'd stayed with Amy for several hours until she finally fell asleep. Afterward, Eric had suggested they get drinks. Nick had agreed because he'd been upset, and he'd been bottling his anger while in Amy's presence. They ended up at Jenkins' on their off day, though the alcohol was heavily discounted for employees. He remembered pouring shot after shot of tequila, straight up. Phil hadn't been around, thank God. After the fifth shot, he didn't remember anything else.

"What time is it?" Nick asked.

"Just past eleven."

Nick's eyes widened. "Shit, I was out that long?" He lunged for his shoes and slipped them on.

Eric frowned in confusion. "What are you in a hurry for? Gotta get back to your rich boyfriend or something?"

"Or something," Nick replied absentmindedly. He'd completely forgotten his plans with Claude that day. "Where's my phone?"

Eric shrugged. "I ain't its fucking keeper."

Nick bit his lip, refraining from saying anything about his friend's smartass retort. He didn't know why, but every time he mentioned Claude, Eric got pissed. Nick retrieved his phone from his coat pocket. There were five missed calls. All from Claude.

Shit, he was dead.

Nick slipped on his coat, pulling up the hood. "Thanks for taking care of me, but I've gotta go. I'll see you tomorrow?"

Eric gave Nick a handshake-slash-pat on the back. Up close like that, Nick noticed the circles under Eric's eyes. Was the guy having trouble sleeping? Maybe he was hitting the weed too hard, too often.

"Yeah, bro. Tomorrow. Want me to call a cab for you?"

"I'll take the bus."

"All right. Be easy, be safe."

Nick inclined his head before he left Eric's apartment.

It took nearly twenty minutes to get to Claude's penthouse by bus. The entire way there, all Nick thought about was how Claude would react to being blown off. What he would say once he learned he'd been around Eric. Like Eric, Claude got pissed at any mention of his friend's name. No matter how many times Nick explained to him that Eric was only a friend, Claude didn't listen. He was a suspicious-as-hell person.

Nick took the elevator up to Claude's floor. He attempted to come up with some sort of excuse to feed him about his absence and noncommunication, but his head hurt too much. Besides, he was at fault so he would apologize, take the verbal lashing, and be done with it.

Nick exhaled a deep breath and stepped inside. The place was dark, except for a single light somewhere near the kitchen. There was no music playing, no TV on, nothing. Just a whole lot of dark and quiet. The exotic scent of Turkish tobacco floated on the air, growing stronger with each footstep toward the kitchen.

Claude sat alone at the dining room table, cigarette in hand, gaze locked on Nick.

Nick swallowed. The man made an imposing sight, sitting there directly beneath a single overhead light, dressed impeccably besides the disheveled tie. His eyes appeared dark. Sinister. The only sounds he made were the light puffs of air on each exhale. Smoke clouded his features.

Nick broke the tense silence first. "Sorry I'm home late. I forgot about our plans."

Claude didn't say anything. He puffed on his cigarette and continued to stare at Nick, making him feel like a freak show on display.

Nick unzipped his coat. "You're not gonna say anything?"

"Where were you?"

Nick glanced at him, surprised to hear his low, steady voice. Honestly, he'd expected Claude to give him the silent treatment. Nick cleared his throat. "You know where I was. Sorry I missed your calls, too. I turned my cell phone off in the hospital and forgot to turn—"

The chair clanging against the marble floor as it fell down shut him up midsentence. Claude approached him with a slow, methodical gait. A predator's walk.

Nick stared at him, his mouth gone dry. As if sensing something dangerous about the man, Nick's body bristled, preparing itself for a fight-or-flight reaction. It took a lot of effort to stand still. To stay calm.

Claude loomed over Nick, staring down his nose at him. Without the smoke distorting his features, Nick noticed how pissed the guy really was. "I didn't know they served alcohol in hospitals," Claude said. "Where were you really? Don't lie to me."

"I *was* at the hospital," Nick said, "but I went to the bar after that."

"With that bartender friend of yours?"

Nick didn't comment. It was true, but somehow he knew admitting it would make things worse.

Claude's nostrils flared with anger. His fists clenched at his side. "You told me you were going alone."

"I went alone, Claude. Eric showed up later. He wanted to see Amy, too, apparently." Nick shook his head, wanting to tear his hair out in frustration. Why were relationships so damn complicated? "Look, I was in a bad mood. That's why I forgot. Seeing Aims sick and in pain...it did something to me. Eric suggested going to a bar to take my mind off things. I got drunk. He took me to his place so I could sleep it off. That's it. Nothing else happened."

Claude's eyes narrowed. "Are you lying to me again?"

"Nothing happened," Nick repeated, anger evident in his voice. "I got up, got on a bus, and came home. I don't care if you don't believe me."

"You took the bus home rather than call Frances?"

Nick shrugged. Truthfully, calling Frances hadn't even crossed his mind. He still wasn't used to being chauffeured around. "It's late. I didn't want to disturb anyone. Besides, I can get around without a damn driver. I am a man, in case you forgot."

Claude growled. "That's not the point. How many times must I tell you not to take the bus? That it isn't safe?"

Nick took a step back, eyes wide with surprise at Claude's sudden outburst. "You know what? I don't need to take this shit from you. I'm leaving."

"Don't you dare."

Nick spun on his heel and headed for the entryway. He was too tired, too pissed, and in too much pain to deal with Claude's mood swings. He zipped up his coat at the elevator.

Claude suddenly gripped his wrist, startling him. Nick's back hit the wall before he registered what had happened. Claude pinned him against it, his face twisted in anger.

Nick swung at him, but Claude caught his fist before he made contact. They tumbled to the floor in a heap with Claude on top, using his strength advantage to hold Nick down.

"Get the fuck off me," Nick shouted. He fought and struggled, but Claude wouldn't budge.

Claude ripped open Nick's coat and thrust his hand beneath Nick's sweatshirt, his clammy palm skimming Nick's stomach.

Nick froze. "What are you doing?"

Claude ignored him. He trailed his fingers across Nick's chest, his expression deranged in the moonlight spilling in through the open curtains. He latched onto Nick's left nipple, giving the nub a hard squeeze.

Nick winced at the small stab of pain, but his cock jerked in reaction.

"You're mine," Claude whispered harshly. "Did you really think I would let you go so easily?" He reached for Nick's belt buckle.

Nick grabbed his wrist. "Stop."

Claude pressed his lips against his, kissing him hard enough to bump teeth. He shoved his tongue inside, tilting his head back to thrust as deep as possible. The aggression he used was as if he wanted to choke him with a kiss.

Nick's eyes watered. Grabbing a fistful of Claude's hair, Nick pried his mouth away. "I said stop."

Claude's lips eased into a smirk. "Oh, Christian." He buried his face into the hollow of Nick's throat. "You don't want to know what I'll do if you leave me again."

Chapter Fourteen

"HANNAH CALLED. I need to make a stop at the office first, if you don't mind."

Nick peered at Claude through the bathroom mirror where they primped for their brunch date. His lover finger-combed his freshly cut dark-blond locks into place. He ran a hand over his recently shaved chin for stubble, but there wasn't any. His face looked as smooth as a baby's bottom.

"I don't mind," Nick answered. He smoothed down his wool sweater.

Claude leaned in close and planted a kiss on Nick's cheek. "It shouldn't take long. Once I check things there, I plan to treat you to the best French cuisine you've ever had."

Nick gave a half-hearted smile. He'd never eaten French food anyway, unless french fries counted. Regardless, it didn't matter. Ever since that night a week before when he'd gotten drunk and forgotten about their plans, Nick hadn't been able to interact with Claude normally.

Claude had brushed the entire thing under the rug. But Nick hadn't. The Claude he'd seen that night was nothing like the Claude he was used to most days. That Claude was dangerous. Deranged. Without a doubt, the guy could do the unthinkable if pushed hard enough.

A niggling part of Nick knew he should get out while he was able, but he couldn't force himself to leave. Claude had been kind since the beginning. He'd allowed him to stay in his home, took care of him, worried over his safety, and spoiled him with the kind of luxury Nick had only ever dreamed about. Oh, and there was also the one little fact that Nick was starting to fall for the guy. At least, he thought so. He'd never had these feelings for anyone else before and Claude was his first-ever boyfriend. Nick couldn't help wanting to stay and help Claude like Claude helped him.

"Are you ready to go, *mijn lief?*"

Nick raked a hand through his tousled dark locks, not fretting about his appearance as much as Claude had. "Yeah." He took Claude's outstretched hand, letting the older man lead him outside.

Nick expected Frances to be waiting for them with the Bentley. Instead, Claude ushered him inside his Ferrari. "I'm in the mood to drive today."

"Cool."

Unlike the day of their yacht excursion, it was freezing cold out. Though Nick had bundled up, the frigid air penetrated his bones. They drove across town with the windows up, heat blasting, and Nick's favorite hip-hop music playing. A half hour later, Claude pulled into the parking lot of a huge building that was all modern and artsy and elegant. The entire front was made of some sort of reflective glass.

Claude stepped outside first and opened the door for him.

Nick's face flushed. "Thanks." He followed Claude to the door where he used a security card to get inside. The lobby was huge, yet modern and simple. The gleaming marble floors reflected the bright overhead lights, making it appear to have more wattage than there actually was. A station was set up with a brunch feast perfect for early mornings and late afternoons before dinner. Nick's mouth watered at the strong scent of roasted coffee.

"Mr. Vanderpoel."

Nick turned around to spot a beautiful young woman approaching, tall and slim like a runway model. She wore her long blonde hair in a style similar to the women from *Mad Men*. Nick had no clue what designer dress she had on, but she looked good in it. Cutouts in the right places. A modest slit in the side. The woman walked with confidence, as if aware of being hot stuff.

Claude smiled when she stopped at his side. "Hannah. Off to lunch?"

"Yes, sir." She took off her sunglasses and stared at Nick with gold-lidded brown eyes.

"You remember Ober Hannah, don't you?" Claude asked him.

Nick gave a reluctant nod. He'd never met that woman in his entire life.

Hannah beamed. "It's so good to see you. You have no idea how glad I am that you're here. Claude is a happy man because of you."

"Thanks." Nick shuffled his feet. The situation was getting uncomfortable fast.

Hannah's gaze lingered on him briefly before she faced Claude. "Sorry to ruin your plans, but I emailed you the details. If you'll confirm everything for me, you can be on your way."

"Not at all." Claude glanced at Nick. "Care to accompany me?"

Nick shook his head. "I'll stay in the lobby 'til you're done."

"All right, then. I won't be long." Claude kissed his hand in an overly romantic and embarrassing gesture. He gave Nick a mischievous parting smile as he strode off toward his office.

Sighing, Nick turned around. Hannah was staring at him again. The friendliness she'd worn moments before had disappeared, replaced by confusion.

Nick offered his hand. The one Claude hadn't kissed. "I'm Nick, by the way. We've never actually met."

Hannah didn't take it. She glared at him, her upper lip curled. "Of course not. I knew the real Christian, and I know that you are not him."

Nick stiffened at her words and what they implied. The real Christian?

Before he could say anything, however, she retreated. Headed to lunch somewhere. Nick slumped into the nearest chair, racked with disbelief. That was it the entire time. The reason why Claude had helped him; the reason why he acted as if they'd known one another for years. He thought Nick was someone else. Not because he liked Nick, or even saw him for that matter.

Nick slammed his fist against the armchair. Pain spread through his palm. "I'm such a fucking idiot."

Not like he hadn't had his suspicions in the beginning, anyway. Caught up in his own feelings for the guy, he'd pushed them into the background.

Claude reappeared not five minutes after Hannah left.

"That was fast," Nick said.

"I can be quick when it counts. Come." This time when Claude offered his hand, Nick didn't take it.

CLAUDE DROVE DOWNTOWN, bound for a French restaurant called Lafayette. Nick hadn't heard of it. They drove in silence, as if Claude sensed Nick's sudden shift in mood and had given him time to clear his head. It'd helped calm him somewhat.

Claude parked the car. "If you'd rather we ordered in, I'd be fine with that."

"Anyone ever tell you you're too fucking considerate sometimes?"

Claude arched a brow, confused by his sudden behavior. "Not in the way you're phrasing it, no."

"I mean, I don't get you. Here I am, ruining your good mood with my shitty attitude, yet you're still thinking about what *I* want. There's something seriously wrong with you." Nick sank against the leather passenger seat and gazed out the window. Regret churned in his gut. He didn't want to take his temper out on Claude like that, but he had no one else to blame. That way seemed easier, and didn't that make him a goddamn coward?

"Look at me."

The demanding tone made Nick's head snap back in Claude's direction. He stared into Claude's stern face, his breathing heavy. "What?"

Claude cupped his cheek, startling him. Nick expected him to go off about his *mis*behavior. Instead, those eyes appeared soft as he searched Nick's expression. "You've no idea how empty I was after you left. But it's because of you that I'm whole now. Because of you I can genuinely smile again. That's why I'd do anything for you. I'd do *anything* to keep you safe right beside me." Something flashed on his face. Pain, maybe? Regret? Whatever it was, the emotion vanished as quickly as Nick had realized it. "I love you, Christian."

Nick winced. For a second there, he'd almost allowed himself to believe Claude was actually talking about him.

Claude brushed their lips together. His were slightly cold and moist.

Nick didn't hesitate to kiss him. That, he could do. Everything else might be muddled and frustrating, but that was easy. Straightforward.

Only a hint of Claude's tongue entered his mouth, but it was enough for Nick to suck and savor. Claude's velvety tongue tasted like spice from the cigarette he'd smoked earlier that morning. Nick slid his tongue into Claude's mouth and kissed him deeper. Claude reciprocated.

After what seemed like forever, Claude pulled away, just enough that their foreheads still touched. His warm breaths fell on Nick's skin. "If you want, we could go home. I wouldn't have any objections."

Nick shook his head. "You came all this way. Besides, I'm starving."

Claude retreated from him, his eyes glossy with lust. "I suppose there is always time for dessert later." They exited the car and Claude led him inside the restaurant.

Nick gaped as he admired the space. Lafayette wasn't just a restaurant. It was a boulangerie and bakery, according to the words on the window. The inside was impressive. Mingled aromas of different meats and sweets wafted into his nose. A rotisserie counter stood beside them at the entryway. Seasoned skewered chicken rotated on a spit.

A hostess wearing a black dress and white pearl necklace greeted them.

"We'd like a booth, please," Claude said.

"Right this way."

As she led them through the main dining room, Nick sensed people's stares on them, but he didn't care. He continued to take note of the European-styled place. The setting was lavish, yet still relaxed. Outside of the Euro flair, the restaurant boasted mahogany floors, fancy murals, and towering arched windows overlooking the street. There were blue and honey-colored tiles designed for intimate spaces. Nick whistled low as they passed by a golden bar with a large glowing clock.

"I feel like I'm in a movie," he said.

Claude chuckled.

The hostess finally placed them at a plush leather booth and gave them menus. "A waiter will be with you momentarily." She left them.

Nick leafed through the menu, trying to find what sounded good. He never used to eat food like this. Not until he met Claude.

As if sensing his uncertainty, Claude said, "The French toast is good, if you prefer something more breakfast-y."

"Thanks, but I recognize what most of this stuff is."

Claude gave an apologetic smile. "I wasn't trying to offend you."

Nick sighed. "My bad. I'm ruining the mood, I know." Even though his anger was justified, he didn't want to hurt Claude or upset him.

Claude placed his hand on top of Nick's. Unadulterated affection gleamed in his eyes. Too bad it wasn't really for Nick. "Don't be sorry," Claude said. "You're not doing anything wrong."

Nick gently pulled his hand away. He leafed through the menu, though Claude's gaze still bored into him like hot lasers. "What is *jus frais?*"

"Fresh juice."

A tall, thin man approached and introduced himself as their waiter.

Nick ordered first. "I'll take the French toast *tropique* with grilled pineapple and a side of bacon *maison*."

"Okay. And for you, sir?"

"I'll take the smoked salmon benedict on brioche, and a side of sausage." Claude handed over their menus.

"Very good. Would you care for our wine list?"

"No, we'll have two Hyper Cs, please."

The waiter finished writing their orders and left them alone.

"What's in that?" Nick asked.

"Blood orange, yuzu, and grapefruit. Trust me, it's delicious."

"Sounds like it." Nick gazed around the restaurant where other well-dressed, bright-eyed patrons dined and chattered in hushed voices. He didn't really focus on them, though. His mind churned with thoughts of getting through to Claude. Of explaining to him he wasn't Christian. Not in the slightest. Things would only get worse if this kept on. Already bad enough Hannah thought he was taking advantage of Claude's misperception.

Nick turned around to find Claude staring at him, hands folded gracefully beneath his chin. The love shining in his direct gaze made it harder for Nick to breathe. "What? I got something on my face?"

Claude shook his head. "No. I never thought I'd see this day again. It still feels like I'm dreaming." The smile dissipated at the edges and Claude's gaze grew hazy, as if he'd suddenly gone somewhere else.

Nick touched Claude's intertwined hands. "You okay?"

Claude blinked rapidly. "I'm fine."

"Hey listen. I need to tell you—"

The sudden eruption of clapping from the table across from them cut Nick's next words. The staff brought out a huge chocolate cake with a sparkler for someone's birthday, apparently.

Claude grabbed his hand, bringing his attention back. "You were saying something?"

Nick licked his lips, his heart racing as he met Claude's eyes. He opened his mouth to speak, but their waiter returned with their drinks.

"Two Hyper Cs," he announced.

"Thank you," Claude mumbled, voice filled with veiled irritation.

What perfect fucking timing...

With a sigh, Nick lifted the glass of cantaloupe-colored liquid that reminded him of carrot juice. He sipped the citrus-scented drink. It slid down his throat, smooth and cold, and somewhat sweet and acidic.

"It's refreshing."

"I figured you might prefer it to green juice."

"Yeah."

Claude set his drink aside and aimed his penetrating gaze on Nick again. "What were you going to tell me?"

Nick took another sip of his drink. That time, it might as well have been water. The moment had passed, and though he wanted to confront Claude about it, he didn't care to dampen the mood. Again. Still, Claude was expecting an answer, so... Nick cleared his throat.

"How would you like to meet Amy today?"

THEY DIDN'T STAY long at Lafayette, maybe an hour, hour and a half tops. Then they were on the road toward the New York Med with a brief stop at a flower stand.

Even though Nick had thrown the suggestion out there as a last ditch move, Claude hadn't reacted the way he'd expected him to. He'd thought the guy would be thrilled.

Instead, Claude only said "All right" in a deadpan tone and hadn't spoken any more about it.

That cucumber-cool attitude made Nick want to rescind the invitation, but he knew how childish that was. Besides, he did still feel bad for telling Claude to stay the hell away from her a few weeks back. Yet another case of him taking his anger out on Claude.

"Is she always in inpatient care?"

Nick frowned at Claude's sudden question. He'd thought Claude was uninterested. "What?"

Claude glanced at him briefly before turning to the road again. "Your sister. Does she live in the inpatient care?"

"No. She gets to go home between treatments."

"Do you ever visit her at home?"

Nick stared out of the windshield, not really seeing anything. "No," he replied, his tone low and bitter. He'd vowed to never step foot inside that house again.

"I see."

Nick sighed with relief when Claude didn't press. Although he'd been there the day Nicole had visited, and it was probably easy to put two and two together, he didn't pry. Nick closed his eyes, gratefulness washing over him. He didn't want to ever get into it, and it would piss him off if Claude asked him to.

Once they arrived at the hospital, Nick got them signed in. Mixed feelings coursed through him as he led Claude down the sterile hallway toward Amy's room. Part of him wanted to turn back around to protect his sister from Claude's presence. He was a side of his life Amy didn't know about, and introducing the two could be a huge statement. One he wasn't entirely ready for.

The other part of him wanted to show a little gratitude for the things Claude had done for him so far. He put one foot in front of the other and continued to her room. Amy would be thrilled. He'd never introduced her to a lover before.

Nick knocked twice on her door. "Aims? I'm coming in." He pushed it open. "I've got someone here who wants to meet you."

Amy sat upright in bed, her arm outstretched for a nurse attaching a blood pressure cuff. Her dark green eyes gleamed when she noticed him. "Nick," she exclaimed with delight, "I didn't know you were coming today."

Nick couldn't help mirroring her infectious expression. "I wanted to surprise you. This is Claude, by the way. He's my—"

"I know," Amy interrupted. "He's your rich boyfriend, right?"

Nick scowled at her. He glanced between the giggling nurse and Claude, who didn't seem fazed by what she'd said. "How do you know that?"

Amy shrugged and looked down her arm at the inflating cuff. "Eric told me the last time he was here. He said he was feeling lonely now since you spent most of your time with your rich boyfriend."

Nick peered at Claude out of the corner of his eye. The calm smile he'd been wearing had faded. Eric again. "He said 'rich boyfriend' as an insult, Aims."

"Oops, sorry. I didn't mean to offend you."

Claude's smile returned. He inched closer to the bed. "It's fine. It's very nice to finally meet you, Amy." He held out the bouquet of brightly colored tulips to her.

"Oh, wow. These are so beautiful, Claude. Thank you."

"Not a problem." He set them on the nightstand beside her.

The nurse wrote the numbers and pulled off the cuff. "Okay, Amy, I'll be back in a few minutes to get blood samples. I'll also put these in some water for you."

"Thanks, Sheila."

After the nurse left, Nick took a seat on the edge of Amy's bed. Besides looking a little tired, his sister appeared fine. "How are you feeling today?"

"I'm better now." Her gaze slid from Nick to Claude and back again, lips pursed and shoulders tightened. She had something to say.

Nick rolled his eyes. "Say it, Amy."

She burst into a fit of giggles, her cheeks flushed from the effort. "This is the first time you've introduced me to someone you were dating. You must *really* like him, huh?"

Nick glanced at Claude, who gave him a wink.

"I hope so," Claude said. "I don't know what I would do if he didn't."

Nick tried not to think about last week and Claude's looming threat. He didn't know and didn't want to know.

Of course, Amy's innocent mind only construed their relationship for how romantic it sounded. How much it supposedly proved Claude loved him. "I'm sure he does. Besides, I like you already, so he has to like you too."

Claude chuckled. "I appreciate it."

"I mean, why else would he introduce you to me?"

Nick didn't comment that there'd never been any past lovers to introduce her to. Only the clients he'd blown and fucked for money, and Amy would never know about that.

"You're really handsome, too. Nothing like what Eric described."

Claude pulled up a chair beside Amy's bed. Even though he wore a cheerful expression, resentment floated behind his gaze. "Oh, really? What did Eric say I looked like?"

Nick tensed. He could only imagine what his friend might have said, given his dislike of the guy.

Amy gave Nick a worried expression. She must have sensed something off. "Um..."

The door opened and a short woman with wild brown curls and deep, dark eyes strode in. Her pink lips were compressed into a thin, tight smile, but Nick didn't take offense. For as long as he'd known her, Dr. Julie Thompson had never been much of a smiler. She'd been through too much in her career. It showed on her lined face and in her hardened gaze.

"How long has it been, Nick?" she said in a low, yet strong voice.

Nick scratched his head. "It's been a while. Sorry about that."

"It's all right, son. I just came to see about my angel, but I didn't expect to find Michael here as well."

"Michael?" Claude asked, confused.

Julie turned to him with questioning brows. "Forgive me for not introducing myself. I'm Dr. Julie Thompson. I'm this little one's caretaker." She gave Amy's shoulder a delicate squeeze.

Claude opened his mouth to speak, but Amy cut him off, "This is Claude, Nick's rich boyfriend."

As Julie's eyes widened slightly, Nick fought down the urge to strangle his little sister for her big mouth. He would never, ever hurt her, though sometimes he really wanted to. Like at that exact moment.

"Thanks, Aims. Really."

Amy grinned, uncaring.

"Why did you call him 'Michael'?" Claude asked.

Nick noted the subtle anger threatening to boil up inside of him. Of course, Claude was already confused about Nick's identity. Adding another name into the mix would probably give him an ulcer.

"It's a nickname," Nick explained. "She's basically saying I'm like Michael, the archangel from the Bible. Even though that's not at all true."

Julie's features softened. "From the moment I first met you, you were your sister's protector and guardian angel. After all this time, you still fit the name to perfection."

Nick's cheeks heated. He didn't feel like the noble knight Julie made him out to be. The fact that he'd left Amy alone with two "parents" he'd despised proved he was a failure. The fact that Amy had gotten sick after he'd left and he hadn't been there for her made his gut churn with guilt.

"You don't have to make me out to be something special," Nick said. "I'm not. She's family, and that's what family does for one another." The impatience in his own voice was clear.

Julie shook her head, her sharp features stern. "Don't downplay the things you've done, Nick. You've gone above and beyond for her. Not every family would do that."

The door opened. Sheila entered with the equipment needed to draw Amy's blood. "Dr. Thompson, I didn't realize you were here. I was just about to take a sample. Are you ready for me, Amy?"

Amy nodded. The girl feared needles, yet she still put on a brave front.

Nick left the room without a word. He didn't watch them draw blood from her. Didn't want to see her obvious pain, though she fought through it anyway. The thoughts alone made him nauseous.

"Christian."

Nick spun around to find Claude standing behind him, his face hard and expressionless. "What?"

"The others are worried about you. So am I."

"What do you think about Dr. Thompson? She's amazing, right?"

Claude hesitated, probably wondering if that was a trick question. "She seems capable."

"Yeah, she's pretty great. Especially with Amy. I wish I had a mom like her, you know? And if not me, then I wish Julie could've been Amy's mom. Then I wouldn't worry about her well-being when she's at home."

"Speaking of Amy..."

Nick glared at the older male, but Claude didn't flinch.

"Why did you hide your sister from me for so long? Why does she also call you Nick?"

Nick closed his eyes against the barrage of questions. He really didn't want to deal with that right then. "What if I told you I'm not who you think I am?" He peered up to find Claude standing in front of him, looming, his hazel eyes almost black. His entire body grew rigid. Claude's aura was toxic.

"What does that mean?" Claude asked in a low voice.

Nick swallowed past the lump in his throat. "Don't worry about it." It didn't matter what he said, anyway. Claude wouldn't believe him unless he had proof he wasn't Christian.

Claude's face softened in reaction to Nick's fear. He placed his hands on Nick's shoulders. "I don't want to dwell on the past. I don't care about what you've done. All I care about is moving forward." Claude kissed the corner of his mouth. "With you." He pressed his lips to his, and then his phone rang. Claude pulled away with a curse and put the phone against his ear.

"What is it, Hannah?"

Hannah...

Nick's eyes widened as a light bulb exploded to life in his head. If anyone could help him figure out what happened to the real Christian, she could.

Chapter Fifteen

CLAUDE WAS TAKING a shower.

It was the perfect opportunity for Nick.

In the bedroom, Claude had left his cell phone on the nightstand to charge. Nick took a moment to scroll through Claude's contacts for Hannah's number. For the life of him, Nick couldn't understand why he didn't lock his phone. Besides a few contacts, Claude didn't use his phone for anything personal. There weren't even any selfies in his photo album.

Nick programmed Hannah's number into his own cell phone, then gave her a call.

She picked up after the first ring. "Who is this?"

Nick arched a brow at her snobbish tone. He wanted to ask if she always answered the phone like that and then remembered he might need her help. Polite it was.

"This is Nick, Claude's—" He hesitated. Was he really Claude's lover if Claude thought he was someone else? He cleared his throat. "We met yesterday."

"I remember. Can I help you with something, Nick?"

"Yeah, remember how you told me you knew the real Christian? I just thought, if it's okay with you, I could ask you some questions about him. And maybe clear up some misconceptions."

There was quiet on the other line.

A full thirty seconds of silence ticked by. Nick wondered if she hung up. He was about to click off when Hannah sighed into his ear. "Okay. Meet me at Central Park in a half hour." The line went dead.

Nick pocketed his phone as the shower went silent. Claude exited the bathroom in a terry cloth robe, towel-drying his dark-blond locks. "Were you talking to someone?"

Nick nodded. "Yeah, I have to go. Meeting a friend."

"Eric?" Claude asked suspiciously.

"I have friends besides Eric, in case you didn't know."

"Make sure you're back by six. I made dinner reservations."

"Will do." Nick headed for the elevator, but Claude pulled him to a stop, spinning him around to face him. He placed a chaste, pleasant kiss to Nick's lips. Nick closed his eyes, allowing himself to melt into Claude without doubts taking over his head.

Claude pulled away first after a long moment. "Do you need to call Frances?"

Nick shook his head. "I won't be too far, actually. Later." He hurried and left the room before they got caught up in other things. He had legitimate questions that needed real answers, and he wouldn't get deterred.

Nick didn't take long to get to Central Park. Not with Claude's penthouse overlooking the entire thing. It was a cold-as-hell day, but other than the freezing temperature, he didn't pay attention to anything else. He walked through the snow-covered park, barely taking in the landscapes, monuments, different bodies of water, or any attractions people loved such as the Belvedere Castle, Gapstow Bridge, or the Shakespeare Garden. His mind was only on finding out about the real Christian.

His phone buzzed with a text from Hannah.

Where are you?

Nick glanced around at the bundled, giggling children and doting parents a few feet away, ice skating on a large rink. The scene of happy families, lovers, and friends gliding on the ice appeared straight out of a movie. *Home Alone 2* came to mind.

Nick texted her back: *Ice skating rink. Wollman.*

Hannah didn't keep him waiting long. As she approached him, she definitely stood out from the rest of the crowd, even though they were in Manhattan. She wore an expensive-looking Russian fur hat paired with big diamond hoop earrings. Her trench coat was red, wool, and European, and she sported red-soled heels despite the slush on the ground. She looked fresh off the runway.

"Thanks for meeting with me," Nick said once she settled beside him, taller in her four- or five-inch heels.

Hannah tucked her black leather-clad hands into her coat pockets. "I should have chosen somewhere warmer."

"Here is good. I didn't want to go too far from the penthouse, anyway. Claude and I have dinner reservations tonight, and I'm still not familiar with this area. Didn't want to get lost or something."

"Well, let's get straight to the point, shall we?"

"Yeah, let's." Nick faced her head-on, steely with resolve. "But first, let me clear up one thing. I'm not taking advantage of the fact Claude thinks I'm Christian, all right? I'm not using him for his money. I'm not stealing from him." Well, that wasn't entirely true, but he'd since apologized and paid him back most of what he owed. And he'd never done it again, either. "I've tried telling Claude a dozen times who I really am, but he won't listen. That's why I came to you for answers."

Hannah observed him with shrewd, lash-fringed eyes. Whether she believed him or not, Nick couldn't tell. Not with her blank expression. "Okay, hypothetically speaking, let's say I do believe you. There's something *I* need to know before I answer all your questions."

Nick braced himself. "Shoot."

"Do you genuinely care for Claude?"

Nick blinked at her, taken aback by the question. Though he should've known. A part of him begged to get defensive, to tell her to mind her own fucking business, but then he'd be worse off than where he'd started.

"Really think about it before you answer," Hannah chided.

Nick thought about it. Claude really was an awesome guy. Good-looking, great in bed, and always considerate of Nick. He gave without asking. The guy would literally do anything for Nick. Besides his jealous antics and that one night...Claude was great.

"I do," Nick answered, voice ragged. Not once in his entire life had he ever admitted to liking someone. It wasn't as hard as he figured it would be. "I like him a lot, more than anyone else. That's why I need him to see me and not this Christian dude."

Hannah's face softened at his revelation. "Okay. What do you need to know?"

Nick crossed his arms. He'd been waiting to ask for a long time. "Who is Christian?"

Hannah sighed wearily. "Damn, I wish we had somewhere to sit."

"That bad, huh?"

"Depends on your definition of bad. I can only tell you what I learned from what Claude's told me and what I've seen. You've probably guessed already that Christian was Claude's lover."

Nick nodded. He'd figured that much, given Claude's dedication to the guy.

"When I first met Christian, they were two years into their relationship. Claude told me he'd come across Christian trying to shoplift from Barney's, and he'd bailed him out. Long story short, Christian tracked him down for whatever reason, and the two ended up seeing each other.

"Claude usually doesn't talk about his personal life, if you didn't notice, since he doesn't get along with his father and hasn't had the happiest of upbringings. But he did talk about Christian."

"Why? What made him so special?" Nick cringed at the jealousy in his voice.

"I don't know," Hannah contemplated. "To be honest, I never liked him. Claude talked about Christian like he was an angel sent from heaven to change his life. I didn't get that impression at all."

"What kind of impression did you get?"

Hannah snorted. "Well first, you should have seen the way he was dressed. Not even making a single dollar to his name, yet wearing a full ensemble from Hugo Boss's spring/summer collection, including this amazing leather pilot jacket. And he was draped in jewelry straight out of Cartier."

Nick smirked. "Must have left quite an impression."

"We were meeting at the Four Seasons for dinner, and Christian waltzes right in like he belonged. He was so full of confidence, so charming, and had this air about him as if he owned the entire first world, even though he only possessed what Claude gave to him."

Nick fixed his gaze on her as the haughtiness in her tone returned. Was that what wealth and privilege looked like? Did she dislike Christian because he acted like he belonged in her world when he didn't? Nick took in his own designer jeans and shirt, both gifts from Claude he wouldn't have dared bought for himself given how expensive they were. Did she feel the same about him?

Hannah continued, "He seemed fine enough, but for some reason, I didn't trust him. Turns out, I was right not to."

"Why not?" Nick asked, forcing himself to focus on one thing at a time. He needed answers, not Hannah's or anyone's approval.

Hannah discharged a cold breath. "As time went on, Claude started complaining about Christian more and more. Not only was Christian stealing from him, he cheated on him repeatedly. He showed off Claude's wealth to potential suitors. Every time Claude confronted him, Christian would threaten to leave, forcing Claude to drop it and essentially deal with it."

Nick frowned. "Wait, pause. You're saying Claude put up with this? Why didn't he just dump Christian's ass?" No way in hell he would deal with a lying, cheating, stealing bastard, no matter how good-looking or good in bed he was.

Hannah smiled sadly. "If you find the light in your darkness, you do everything you can to hold onto it."

"What does that mean?"

"What I'm trying to say is, Claude hasn't exactly had a good life. Sure, he comes from a wealthy family. Sure, he got to do things in his childhood most people only ever dream of, but those are surface benefits. In actuality, his life was already predetermined."

"Predetermined?"

Hannah nodded. "Yes. His father had already decided long ago who and what Claude would be. What schools he would attend, who he'd be allowed to socialize with, what his college major would be, what career path he could choose. Claude didn't even want to take over VBI, but because it's the family business, and his father said so, he was left with no choice."

Nick shook his head in sympathy. Though his own life basically sucked balls, he couldn't imagine living a life being stifled from childhood. "I can only guess at what meeting a guy like Christian did to him. Probably felt like freedom."

"Meeting Christian turned him into a lovestruck fool," Hannah said. "Claude was so obsessed with Christian's carefree ways, and his natural vigor for life. But he eventually lost that spark in his eye for Christian. He started to look more miserable and hurt by the things Christian did to him. Then, finally, after four years of being together, Christian dumped him. He took all of his possessions—everything Claude gave him—and even stole money from him, and left without a word. Claude was devastated."

"Sorry," Nick whispered, even though Hannah wasn't the person he wanted to apologize to. Still, he sympathized for what Claude had gone through with the asshole. No one should ever be callously treated by someone they loved. He knew that firsthand.

"Christian was Claude's first true love. And then the little bastard went missing about a year ago. Claude was inconsolable for a long time. I never understood why Claude acted as if he needed Christian, when in actuality, Christian needed Claude."

Nick shrugged. "You said it yourself."

Hannah's brown eyes narrowed at him. "What's your plan?"

"Excuse me?"

"You did say you wanted for Claude to see you, not Christian. How do you plan to accomplish that?"

Nick chuckled softly. Straight to the *real* point. He admired her directness. "With your help, if possible."

Hannah tilted her head to the side. "My help? Exactly what do you need me to do?"

"You know more about Christian than I do. I was hoping you could help me find out where he might be. I plan on showing Claude proof that I'm not him. And speaking of proof, you got any pictures of him or something?"

Hannah's upper lip curled in disgust. "Ugh, God no. If you're worried how alike you two must look, don't. You look nothing like Christian. Except maybe the height. And you have a similar build. But Christian was a blond with blue eyes. He didn't have your dark brooding features."

Nick swallowed at her words. Blond with blue eyes... It was a start, at least. "So, will you help me?"

"I'll help you. But only because Claude is my friend, and I don't want to see him hurt again."

Nick smiled with relief. "I'll take it."

Chapter Sixteen

CHRISTIAN HAD BEEN sneaking out the past week.

Claude sat at the dining room table, barely touching a light breakfast prepared for him while Vicky and Yesenia tidied the kitchen. His mind raced with turmoil, filled with thoughts of where his newly found lover had been. Was he meeting with a secret lover again? Was he stealing from him?

Just the other day, Claude had caught Christian rifling through his closet, obviously looking for something. When Claude questioned him, Christian said he'd misplaced his favorite sweatshirt.

It'd been a blatant lie, and they both knew it.

At the time, Claude hadn't said anything, though he wished he had. He wished he'd forced him into telling the truth, because ever since then, he'd been uneasy.

Claude rubbed his chin. Thoughts of Eric Ruiz filled his mind. He still wasn't entirely sure the two weren't seeing one another.

"Hey."

Claude pivoted at the sound of Christian's groggy voice. His lover moved to stand beside him, rubbing at his tired eyes.

"Good morning, Señor," Vicky addressed him. "Have a seat. Eat." She set a plate filled with blueberry crepes, smoked bacon, and scrambled eggs in front of him. Yesenia poured a glass of orange juice for him—his preferred breakfast drink.

"Thank you," Christian replied with a polite smile. He took a seat beside Claude.

Claude sipped his lukewarm coffee and watched him. The fork slid between Christian's parted lips, his jaw moving while his teeth worked the food into tiny particles. Claude didn't feel lust in that moment. Only curiosity.

What would it take to ensure Christian continued to stay by his side?

"I'm taking you somewhere once you're done eating," Claude said.

Christian eyed him midbite. "Where?"

Claude forced himself to smile. "It's a surprise."

Christian quickly finished breakfast. Though he tried to hide it, Claude sensed his excitement.

Once they were dressed, Claude called Frances to drive them to the airport where the company jet waited. His father forbade him from using the jet for personal endeavors, but that way would be quicker. He'd deal with Augustus if or when he found out.

Christian stepped out of the car first, a cold gust of wind sending a shiver over him as he ogled the sleek transport. "Are we going on a trip somewhere?"

Claude stood beside him. "A weekend retreat. I thought you might like to get away from this cold."

Christian scowled at him. "Why didn't you tell me? I would've left a contact number with Amy and her doctor."

"Don't worry about that. You can give her a call once we land." Claude held out a hand for him. "Come."

Surprisingly, Christian let Claude lead him inside. It appeared he was growing more comfortable with him.

They relaxed during the nearly five-hour flight. Christian had even fallen asleep. With each passing minute, Claude grew a little more excited. He would have Christian alone for an entire intimate weekend. No work. No Eric. No freezing New York snow. Just them, the beach, and plenty of sun.

Claude woke Christian with a soft kiss to his cheek once they touched down.

Christian blinked tired eyes at him. "Where are we?"

"Come see."

Christian gazed out the window, puzzled by the hot unfamiliar surroundings. "Are we out of the country? Because I don't have a passport."

Claude chuckled. "Already taken care of." He patted his coat pocket. "Now come on."

Going through security was a breeze. Once their passports were checked, the woman said, with a thick accent, "Welcome to Jamaica."

Christian's jaw dropped. He waited until they were out of earshot to say, "Holy shit, Claude, you brought me all the way to Jamaica?"

Claude nodded. "Montego Bay, to be exact." He sensed the sudden change in Christian's demeanor. His lover seemed sad, for reasons unknown to Claude. "What's wrong?" Claude asked.

"Nothing. It's just that...if you'd asked me a year before if I thought I'd *ever* get to travel outside the country, I would've easily said no. Kind of in disbelief right now."

A year before...

The same time Christian disappeared from his life.

Claude attempted to clear his mind of that thought. He led the way outside of Sangster International Airport, instantly greeted by the familiar scent of exotic spices, bay rum, and salty sea air. The sun beamed down on the bustling city, but the temperature wasn't unbearable, thanks in part to the shade of the many fruit and palm trees. Christian glanced around in obvious awe, soaking everything in. A smile graced his lips.

"It's crazy," Christian exclaimed.

"Wait until you see the villa."

However, Claude didn't take him there first. They shed their coats, and Claude drove the rental Jeep to the Shoppes at Rose Hall, a shopping mall he planned to purchase essentials: hats, sunglasses, swimwear, enough light clothing for the weekend, sunscreen, and plenty of bottled water to stay hydrated.

They didn't stay long because apparently Christian had lost his love for shopping in the time they'd been apart.

Once they finished at the Shoppes, Claude took him to Doctor's Cave Beach next, Montego Bay's most famous beach, and also Claude's personal favorite, especially around that time when the crystal waters were at its clearest, reflecting the bright sunlight.

The beach was fairly crowded upon arrival, but that was to be expected. Tourists and locals alike flocked to that place to enjoy the same thing. Claude rented chairs after managing to find a somewhat secluded spot.

"Smells like flowers and suntan lotion here," Christian said. He reclined into his seat, staring out beyond the white sands and turquoise waters.

"Put some sunscreen on if you're going shirtless," Claude warned. "We're much closer to the equator here."

Christian peered at him over his brand-new opaque sunglasses. "Fine." He took the bottle of sunscreen, prepared to pour some into his hands, but paused and directed a mischievous grin at Claude. "Wanna put some on me?"

Claude arched a brow. "If I said no?"

"Your loss."

"We couldn't very well have that, could we?" Claude moved into Christian's chair. His skin glowed from the sun's positive effects. Only a few hours there and already he was soaking it in. Claude slathered the creamy substance onto Christian's lean muscled chest and tight abs, rubbing in smooth circles.

Christian didn't move except for a few deep breaths he took as Claude ran his hands over him.

"Turn around so I can get your back."

Christian obliged. "This is waterproof, right?"

Claude worked the thick cream into his musculature. "Yes, why?"

"Because I wanna feel the water. See the boats up close."

Claude glanced out at the usual sailboats and a cruise ship in the distance. Other visitors were swimming, snorkeling, and enjoying all that Doctor's Cave Beach had to offer. Claude couldn't very well deny Christian the chance to enjoy it all, too.

He pressed a gentle, yet firm hand to the small of his back and kissed between his shoulder blades. "Go have fun."

Christian smiled, his eyes glittering like dark emeralds in the sun's rays. "Will you watch me, perv?" He took off his sunglasses and set them in his chair.

Claude couldn't help smirking at that. "Oh, I'll be sure to get an eye full."

"Then I'd better not lose my shorts." Christian took off before Claude could reply.

Claude returned to his chair with a smile. He didn't get to warn Christian that the place was one of unhurriedness.

"It's fucking warm," Christian shouted the instant his legs disappeared calf-deep beneath the water.

Claude stifled a laugh. A few people nearby gave Christian strange looks for his exuberant behavior, but Claude was certain he didn't care. He relaxed as Christian swam underwater, close to the buoy line. His carefree attitude was one of the reasons why Claude fell for him in the first place.

Christian stared out at the horizon, the passing boats and ships, then glanced back in Claude's direction.

Claude's chest fluttered. Even across the distance, their gazes met. Claude was almost certain Christian watched him, pondering. Or maybe he was taking in the wonderful sights of the flowering trees, palm-lined hills, and long stretches of rolling meadows.

Claude allowed Christian to kill time at the beach, snorkeling underwater to explore the coral reefs and underwater caves. Claude lay back beneath the sun and sipped piña coladas.

Once they left the beach, Claude treated them to a jerk chicken dinner with live reggae music, and later to drinks at Margaritaville. He planned on taking Christian to Gloucester Avenue for souvenir shopping the next day.

The sky was pitch-black when Claude drove him to his private villa, however the island was suitably lit. Christian hung out the side of the window, gazing at every fort, plantation house, and eighteenth-century church they passed in anticipation of Claude's second home.

"Are we there yet?" Christian asked for the third time, his words holding the smallest hint of a slur.

"Almost," Claude assured him. "Did you enjoy yourself?"

Christian grinned at him. "I wish Amy was here. She would love this."

Claude massaged Christian's thigh in a comforting manner. Though he'd only met the young woman once, he wanted more for her than her current predicament. Nothing would make him happier than to be the one to facilitate it for her.

Christian's hand touched his own, forcing back Claude's thoughts of the sickly, yet cheerful girl. "I had fun," Christian said, his expression serious.

"Good. We're home."

Claude drove through the gate of a newly built, elegant villa sitting on two acres of manicured grounds. All on one level, the villa possessed a dramatic fifteen-hundred-square-foot great room with soaring twenty-foot ceilings and fifty feet of sliding glass doors opening up to an expansive covered terrace, heated infinity-edge pool, and private garden. Thanks to his staff, his villa had plenty of luxurious amenities.

Christian hopped out of the Jeep first, while Claude's personal butler came to retrieve their belongings. The residence had been prepared for the evening, with galbanum- and lemon-infused scented candles lit next to the pool's edge. A bottle of wine with two glasses sat on a silver tray atop the outdoor recliner.

"Holy shit," Christian whispered with awe, drinking in the sights around him. "This place is huge."

"Go ahead and look around. I'll be by the bar."

Christian trotted off.

Claude rubbed his stiff shoulders. He hadn't realized how much tension he'd been holding in. Since they'd arrived home, he needed to tell Christian about what he'd done.

The bartender made two of his strongest frozen cocktails at Claude's request. Claude took their drinks to the pool. It was a balmy night with a view of the dark sea from their vantage point.

Christian returned moments later and plopped down beside him. "I've never actually seen those before. Not in person, I mean." He grabbed one of the drinks from Claude and took a long sip.

"What's that?"

"Outdoor shower. Yours is really nice with the stones and trees and torches. And the light makes the water look gold. A golden shower." Christian snickered.

Claude didn't laugh at Christian's juvenile remark. "There's something I need to tell you."

Christian's smile faded. "Why do you look so serious all of a sudden?"

"Do I? It's nothing alarming. It's great news, actually."

"Okay," Christian spoke slowly.

Claude brushed off his dire tone. "I visited Amy at the New York Med the other day."

Christian's face went blank. Of course, anything related to his sister was a touchy subject.

"I spoke with Dr. Thompson, and I told her I'm interested in Amy's expenses."

Christian hesitated, as if his mind was slow to process due to his tipsy state. "What are you saying?"

"I'm saying that from now on, I'll be covering Amy's medical expenses. You no longer need to worry about coming up with the money. That's my responsibility." Though Claude did have other, more beneficial reasons for what he did. "I already set up an account to be billed each month automatically. I told Dr. Thompson not to withhold any groundbreaking treatment, no matter how expensive. Money is no object."

Christian rose abruptly, his cocktail spilling over and staining the white chair cover scarlet. He balled his fists at his side, rage clearly written on his reddening countenance.

Claude frowned in confusion. He reached out for Christian, but thought better of it. What could possibly be wrong?

"Who told you to do that?" Christian asked, voice tight and restrained. "Mr. I-Own-Everything, Money-Is-No-Object. Who told you to fucking do that?"

Claude stood. The conversation was getting out of hand. "I think you've had too much to drink. Let's go inside, all right?"

"Fuck you. Don't touch me," Christian barked. Even in the recessed lighting, Christian's eyes glowed like hot magma under the scrutiny of his wrath. "Amy is *my* responsibility, not yours! The only one who's gonna take care of her is me!" Christian shoved him into the chair and stormed off into the villa.

Claude stared at his pleated linen khakis, at the growing red stain spreading from his thigh to seam, the color resembling blood. He'd only been hoping to ease some of the burden from his lover's shoulders. He thought Christian would be pleased. Claude reached inside his breast pocket for a cigarette, his hand trembling. He retrieved the lighter from his pants pocket and lit the tobacco. The strong foreign herbs and spices warmed his insides like a roasting furnace. Claude exhaled a calming breath.

He thought Christian would love for him to spend money for his sister's care. Surely that was why he'd told Claude about her treatments, after all.

"Sir? Sir?"

Claude peered up at the strong, accented voice of his butler. The robust Jamaican native stood over him with a concerned frown.

"I'm sorry?" Claude asked.

"I said that I could clean this mess for you."

Claude hadn't realized he'd spaced out. He looked over the area, and indeed, it was a mess. One blood-red cocktail stained him and his recliner's cover, while the other had spilled out onto the ground in a melted slush. Claude hadn't noticed the glass break, too stunned by Christian's reaction.

Claude sat up straighter, attempting to look composed, though turmoil filled him. "Yes, that will be fine." He stood, looking around for an ashtray. He'd neglected to bring one, though smoking hadn't been on the itinerary for that evening.

His butler took the stub and put it out in the trash receptacle he'd brought along.

"Thank you. Is Christian still inside?"

"Your guest is in the master bathroom, sir."

Claude inclined his head before retreating inside, barely glancing at the table tennis, billiards, and cricket, games he'd thought Christian might enjoy. Soft calypso music streamed into the house via the Sonos system. On autopilot, Claude followed the sound of running water until he entered the master bathroom. The en-suite facility was dark, with lit tea candles surrounding the filled Jacuzzi bathtub, prepared the way Claude had requested.

Christian wasn't in the Jacuzzi. He stood inside the walk-in shower, naked, though obscured by the steam fogging the glass door. His head was down, being soaked through by the double rain-shower heads. He didn't look up at the sound of Claude's approaching footsteps. Whatever plagued his mind, he apparently didn't hear him.

Claude toed off his shoes. He peeled off his soiled pants and shirt and joined Christian in the shower. Steam blasted him and slowed his breathing. The heat was almost unbearable.

Christian didn't move, not even when Claude lathered a bathing sponge with hibiscus-scented bodywash and slid the pouf across his back. "I'm sorry," Claude said. "I can see now that I overstepped my boundaries. I should not have made the decision without your permission."

Christian glanced over his shoulder, his forest-green gaze tormented. "I'm the one who should be apologizing. I get it, man. You were only trying to help. And here I am acting like a rude little bitch who can't hold his liquor. It's just..."

Claude passed the sponge across his lover's chest. "It's just?"

"I'm a joke for ever thinking I can become Amy's guardian. I mean, look at me. I can't even take care of myself. What am I supposed to do with a sick sixteen-year-old? You'd be better off as her caretaker than me. You can do more for her than I ever could."

Claude hesitated at the bitterness in Christian's tone. He knew those words weren't true. There were many things Christian had done—sacrificed—for Amy's sake. There would be no real reasoning for him, however. Not like this.

"Is that what you want?" Claude asked.

Christian didn't answer.

"If it helps, I'll stop payment on her medical bills. I never should have convinced Dr. Thompson in the first place. But she also recognized what you were going through; how hardworking you were. She thought it would help."

Christian shook his head. The resignation in his body conveyed his disappointment. "I can't seem to escape that fucking title."

"What's that?"

"I'm everybody's charity case. Been that way my entire life, and I'm sick of it."

Claude spun Christian around to face him. He pressed his back against the heated slab of marble, looming over his smaller lover. A flash of fear crossed Christian's features, but it disappeared a moment later, replaced by a tough-as-nails mien. Claude hated to appear threatening, but he would do whatever was necessary to make a point.

"You never have been, nor will you ever be my charity case, understand? The things I do for you are out of the love I have for you, not because of obligation or pity." He tightened his grip on Christian's shoulders, desperate to make sure his lover never misunderstood his intentions again. "Do you hear me? I said I love you."

"I hear you," Christian whispered, barely audible over the downpour. "And I'm sorry."

"It's all right." Claude eased him into his arms. Weight lifted from his shoulders as Christian held him back. "Tomorrow is a new day. A new start. For us both."

Chapter Seventeen

THE JET LANDED in New York sometime in the afternoon. When they exited, the sun beamed onto Nick's skin. Spring was right around the corner, and the days were already getting hotter. Still, it didn't compare to the heat of the Jamaican sun. After their first disastrous night in Montego Bay, things had gotten better. They'd done touristy things like shop for souvenirs on the Hip Strip, taste rum at the Appleton Estate, and learned about Annie Palmer at the Rose Hall Great House. They'd literally left with nothing two days before, and now they carried bags filled with stuff upon their arrival, including more rum and Jamaica Blue Mountain coffee.

The only downside to the previous day was Hannah's call about Christian. Apparently, the guy's family had reported him missing nearly a year back. They'd told the police that though Christian frequently ran off with lovers, never had he been gone that long without a word. So far, the police hadn't found him.

Nick was pretty sure Christian was dead.

Frances greeted them with the car and helped load their things into the trunk. "Enjoy your trip, sir?" he asked Claude.

Claude smiled at Nick. "It was refreshing."

Nick agreed. He hadn't realized how much he needed a vacation. He slid into the back seat of the Bentley coupe when his phone beeped. It was a text from Eric:

Where u at?

He'd barely finished reading, when he received another text message. Also from Eric:

U Coming in?

"Eric again?"

Nick turned to see Claude frowning at his phone.

"He's been texting you all weekend."

Nick shrugged. "Yeah, he's worried because I up and left without a word." He sent Eric a text back:

Just got back. TTYL.

"I wonder why." Claude buckled himself in and glared straight ahead, his face set in stone.

Anger boiled in Nick at the implication in Claude's tone. "What's that supposed to mean?"

Frances took off. If he sensed the sudden tension in the car, he didn't react to it.

Claude aimed a harsh stare at Nick. "You know very well what it means. Why else would he be calling your phone all weekend if the two of you were not intimately involved in some way?"

Nick attempted to calmly count to ten in his head, but he seethed inside. He couldn't believe Claude was pulling that shit after the great day they'd had. He only made it to seven, and his temper won out.

"I'm sick of your jealousy, Claude. I mean, really? How many times I gotta tell you? No, I'm not fucking my best friend."

"Of course not," Claude said, his tone dripping sarcasm.

"Whatever." Nick didn't have time for this.

Frances drove quicker than usual because they made it back to the penthouse in record time. Nick hopped out of the car before Frances put the thing into park. He stormed inside and grabbed his uniform.

Claude appeared in the bedroom just as Nick pulled off his shirt. "Where are you going?"

"Work." He didn't need to be there for another two hours, but he'd rather get there early than deal with Claude like that. "I can't deal with your jealousy."

"I want you to quit your job."

Nick frowned. "Excuse me?"

"I have more than enough money to take care of you for the rest of your life. There's no reason for you to continue employment in that place."

Nick stared at him with wide eyes, incredulous. Was Claude for real? Did he really expect Nick to just up and quit his job and rely on him for everything? "No."

Claude arched a brow at him. "No?"

"Hell no," Nick said. "If you expect me to lay up on you and your money for the rest of my life, then you don't know shit about me."

Claude gave him a bitter smile. "Or is the real reason why you won't quit because you won't see Eric again?"

Nick shook his head. He was through with the discussion. "I'm done." He headed for the elevator, but Claude blocked his way. Nick glared at him. "Move."

"Watch yourself," Claude said in a low voice. "I don't trust Eric. He wants you. He'll do anything to have you."

"Move," Nick repeated, refusing to go where Claude wanted him to go. Eric was his friend. His brother. He trusted him implicitly.

Claude initiated a tense stare-off between them, his gaze so intense Nick yearned to look away. He held his ground. No one was going to intimidate him ever again.

Finally, Claude relented and stepped aside. Nick brushed past him without a second glance.

NICK TOOK HIS time getting to work, though once he got there, he still had about an hour before his shift started.

Phil wasn't on the stage playing the saxophone like usual. Instead, he managed the chefs in the kitchen, preparing for the night. Outside of them, no one else was around. The entire dining room was empty. Nick took a seat at the bar, placing his forehead against the cool ebony wood. Doubt filled his mind. Doubt about his "relationship" with Claude. He knew people had their hang-ups, but Jesus Christ, that was too much. Worse still, he didn't know how to deal with it. Not like he ever had a jealous lover before.

"Someone looks like he needs a drink."

Nick peered at Eric's smirking mug. He didn't look as pissed off as Nick expected, but his eyes weren't too happy, either. "What's up?"

"What's up? Is that all you gotta say to me after avoiding my calls all weekend?"

Out of respect for Claude.

He realized how stupid that had been. "I'm sorry."

Eric's features softened with concern. "It's cool, bro." His friend moved behind the bar. He filled two shot glasses with Hornitos Lime Shot tequila and handed one to Nick.

Nick frowned at the crystal clear liquid. "We're on the clock, dude."

"I didn't clock in yet. Did you?"

Nick shook his head.

"Then drink up." Eric clinked the small glasses together and downed his shot with an audible gasp.

Nick put the cup to his mouth, inhaling the sweet citrus and agave aroma. He swallowed the sour and bitter concoction with a cough.

Eric grinned. "So where were you anyway?"

Nick slid over his glass, and Eric poured another shot. He drank it all, tasting the sweet, then salty, entry that time. He wiped his lips. "Jamaica."

Eric guzzled another one. "For real? He took you to Jamaica?"

"Yep, on a weekend retreat."

"How was it?"

Nick smiled at the memory of the past two days. Despite what had happened, he'd still enjoyed his time there. "Hot. Beautiful. We stayed in Montego Bay, and it was amazing."

"I hear that. I'm long overdue for a vacay, yo." Eric put away the glasses and tequila, and wiped the counter. "I'm going down to Miami this summer. Got some friends out there. It's gonna be one huge-ass party, *hermano*. Talking 'bout drinking, girls in thongs on the beach, hitting up nightclubs, whatever. Sky's the limit. I was gonna ask you to come with me, but..."

"I'll come." Why the hell wouldn't he?

"You sure? Upper East Side won't mind?"

Nick scoffed. "I'm supposed to care if he does or doesn't?"

"Oh shit, what happened?"

Nick opened his mouth to speak, but Phil appeared from the back. He nodded at them in greeting as he headed to the stage to play. Nick shook his head. "Let me come to your place after work and I'll tell you."

THEIR SHIFT ENDED at two in the morning. Nick vented to Eric about Claude's jealousy while they drove Eric's friend's car to the liquor store near Eric's apartment before heading home.

Nick was tired as hell, but he didn't want to go home to Claude. Looking at his face would only piss him off more.

Eric carried in the brown-bagged bottles. He nudged Nick's shoulder. "Wonder what he would *really* do if it were true. I'm just saying, you and I should fuck for real. Give him a reason to be jealous."

"Maybe we should," Nick mumbled. He didn't really mean it, though. He wasn't a cheater, and besides, he and Eric were too much like brothers. Nick couldn't imagine ever going there with him.

Eric let them inside and switched the light on. His apartment was perpetually bathed in the scent of marijuana since Eric hit the stuff on a regular basis.

Eric strode into the kitchen. "You hungry? I got some chili."

"I'm good." Nick took a seat on the sofa and uncapped his beer. The PlayStation was on, *Grand Theft Auto* on pause. Eric loved his video games. Nick grabbed the controller to continue where Eric left off. He needed the distraction.

In the distance, Eric lit up and inhaled a deep puff of the strong smoke. The microwave came on, followed by the scent of chili beans and Tabasco sauce.

A few minutes later, Eric set a steaming bowl in front of him. "Here, man. You need to eat something. Don't just drink, straight up."

"Thanks." He set down the controller and picked up the bowl. Steam wafted into his nose. It smelled amazing.

Eric took a seat beside him with his own chili bowl and the lit joint between his lips. "Take it."

Nick took the marijuana, inhaling a deep drag. He didn't enjoy the stuff, though the few times he'd smoked it, he felt good. At that moment, he really needed to feel good.

While Eric played the game, Nick's gaze skimmed over his friend's thick, muscled arms. He was covered in ink, most of them black due to Eric's dark-olive skin tone. Some of the tattoos looked familiar, like the Santa María—representative of Eric's Catholic upbringing—and Palo Alto, Eric's hometown. There were names written in fine cursive print, surrounded by angel wings. Most likely names of fallen friends or family. Other tattoos were phrases written in Spanish, and painted on his upper right bicep was a kickass skull for *Día de los Muertos*—Day of the Dead.

Eric grinned at him. "Like what you see?"

Nick nodded. "Just admiring your tats. Wonder what some of them mean. Like this one." He pointed to a tattoo on his wrist that read LG4L in bold 3D print.

Eric gazed down, his body wired. He shook his head. "It's for my little brother, back in California. Just something he always said."

"Uh-huh." Nick didn't entirely believe him, but he dropped the subject. It wasn't any of his business anyway.

The next few hours flew by in a blur. A drunken, laughter-riddled blur. They talked, smoked, drank, and played games. Nick allowed himself to live in the moment and not think about anything else.

Eric finished off another beer and belched. He giggled, face red, as if burping was the funniest thing in the world.

Nick shook his head. "I'm so fucking tired right now. What time is it?"

"I don't—hold on. Hold on." Eric reached for his phone on the coffee table. He stumbled and fell on his ass, his face pressed into Nick's thigh. He laughed even harder.

Nick shoved at him, though he couldn't help laughing either. "What's wrong with you? I thought you could hold your alcohol better than this."

"It ain't just the alcohol, *ése. Estoy drogado.*"

"You're high. I get it." Nick grabbed Eric's phone. "Holy shit, it's after seven. I gotta get back." A shudder crawled down his spine as he remembered the last time he'd stayed over at Eric's place without telling Claude. He did *not* desire a repeat of that.

Nick stood up to leave, but Eric pulled him down. "Where you going?"

Nick gripped the armrest of the sofa to keep from falling. Jesus, the guy was strong. "I'm tired, man. I need to go home."

"Stay here. Stay the night with me. I'll take care of you."

Nick peered into eyes darkened with lust. The friends-shooting-the-shit aura had changed into something completely different. "Eric, dude—"

Eric didn't listen. He yanked Nick down until he practically fell into his lap.

"Eric, what are you doing? Quit messing around."

"Ain't messing around, Nick. *Me gustas.*" He leaned in close, his lips brushing Nick's earlobe. "*Me gustas mucho, hermano.*"

"What are you—"

Eric pressed his lips against his, silencing his words with a hard kiss.

Nick stiffened, too stunned to move or react. His lips had been parted midspeech, and Eric took advantage by thrusting his alcohol-soaked tongue into Nick's mouth. He tasted like what Nick guessed a bad boy would taste like: bitter and strong, like a human ashtray. The taste of uncultivated spices lay beneath that. It wasn't entirely unpleasant. Not more than the fact his best friend was doing that to him. Nick shoved him away, a little rougher than he meant to. He wiped at his mouth, instantly sobered by the kiss.

Eric's eyes fluttered open to stare at him, maybe processing his reaction a little slower than normal.

"What the hell, man?"

"My bad, Nicky." Though Eric gave him a questioning look, Nick wondered if he was really sorry. He didn't seem to be. In fact, Eric looked like he was prepared to go into Plan B for how to seduce him.

Nick shook his head, refusing to contemplate it. "I gotta go."

"Sure you don't need a ride?"

"Neither of us can drive right now. We're kind of fucked up. We're not thinking clearly."

Eric stroked his goatee, looking as if Nick's words were sinking in. "That's true."

Nick hoped so. He didn't know what to do with Eric's confession. Didn't know if he could continue to be his friend if it was true. "I'll see you later?"

"Yeah, bro. Later. Be careful out there."

"Always."

Chapter Eighteen

CHRISTIAN HADN'T COME home.

Claude checked the stainless-steel Opal clock mounted above his black filing cabinet. Eight o'clock. He hadn't heard a word from Christian since their argument yesterday.

Claude filled his highball glass with more Kentucky bourbon and drank. Six hours earlier, Claude had gone to Christian's job. He'd waited outside for over half an hour when Christian finally appeared with Eric at his side. The two had been intimately sharing conversation before climbing into a car and driving off together. Claude had possessed half a mind to tail them, but surprisingly he hadn't. He'd wanted to trust Christian. Allowing him to drive off unbothered with Eric had been the hardest thing he'd ever done. But he'd done it, despite the doubtful words filling his head. Images of Christian fucking Eric. Of Christian lying beside him in bed, postcoital, sharing laughter, sweet nothings, and kisses. Images of Christian never returning.

Claude had put his trust in his lover and driven home to get some work done. Aside from the one phone call to Vicky, canceling that day's duties, he'd been staring at his Mac notebook ever since.

"Christian is gone," his mind continued to whisper to him. "He's left you. Again."

"No," Claude replied. Christian wouldn't do that again. Not after everything Claude had done for him. There was a reason why Christian wasn't home yet. Why he was still with Eric.

Claude drank more bourbon, the fire in his gut long subsided while he'd continued to drink. He slammed the glass onto the marble desk.

Where was he?

The front door suddenly opened, like an answer to his prayers. "You see, Christian came back," Claude whispered to his inner doubts. He waited for that feeling of elation to course through his veins. To propel him from his seat and into his lover's arms. Strangely enough, it never came. Instead of exuberance, Claude was left boiling. As if the heat of the bourbon had decided to slow roast his insides.

"Claude," Christian's voice called from the hallway. A moment later, the door opened, plunging his room in light. Claude's eyes stung from the brightness.

Christian stood in the doorway, a puzzled expression on his tired face. Claude frowned. Even from there, the stench of alcohol seeped from his pores.

"What are you doing sitting in the dark?" Christian asked.

Claude stared at him. "I was getting some work done," he deadpanned. He'd powered his Mac on but never made it past the home screen. "Why are you home so late? Or is this early?"

"Why are your eyes so red?"

Claude clenched the glass. "Answer the question."

Christian walked farther into the room, shedding his puffer coat. "I was upset about our argument, so I went to Eric's house and we had a few drinks."

Claude's nose wrinkled at the pungent, earthy aroma clinging to him. "It seems to me you had more than a few drinks. Last I checked, recreational use of marijuana was illegal in New York."

Christian frowned. "So?"

Claude's grip on the glass loosened. He reclined back in his leather chair, though he never took his gaze off of him. "So, I guess I shouldn't worry about you upholding any laws. You were a thief when I first met you, after all."

Christian's expression morphed into outrage. "I apologized for that. What else do you want me to do? Get on my knees and beg for your forgiveness? Yeah, right."

"No." Claude rose as his own fury mounted. "I would ask that you remember who I am. Remember that what you do reflects poorly on me. Come home at a reasonable damn time, and for the love of God, stop fucking around on me. That's all I ask. I think I deserve at least that after everything I do for you."

"Fuck around on you? Is that what you think happened? We got drunk. We smoked some pot. That's it. Nothing happened. Get it through your thick skull, dude."

Claude shook his head, refusing to believe that during the hours he'd been gone, nothing had occurred. "Don't lie to me. Something happened."

"Jesus fucking Christ, nothing—" Christian stopped suddenly, his eyes big and glossy, as if his mind had gone somewhere else. He pressed his finger to his lips, rubbing them softly. He lowered his head, unable to meet Claude's gaze.

Realization dawned on Claude. His body stiffened. Christian's expression was all the answer Claude needed. "You little slut."

Christian's head shot upward, his eyes wild and dark with rage. "What did you call me?" He closed the distance between their heated bodies, trembling like a volcano ready to erupt. "What the fuck did you call me?"

Christian shoved at him, but Claude caught his wrist in a tight grip. "Not this time," he whispered.

Christian clenched his teeth. He pulled back his fist, prepared to strike, but Claude dodged the oncoming blow.

"Motherfucker," Christian cried out. "You stupid son of a bitch!" He swung at him, shattering the bourbon glass in the process.

Claude leapt back and out of reach, dodging his punches with mere distance management. With the strength and fury Christian directed at him, he might have been good in a street fight against some untrained rat. Not against Claude. Not only was he trained to shoot, Claude had learned hand-to-hand combat and self-defense techniques at a young age.

Christian threw a right for his head. Without much thought, Claude turtled up so that Christian's punch ricocheted off his arm. Claude wrapped his arm around Christian's, above the elbow, and held on tight, neutralizing the limb.

Christian struggled to get free. "Get off me."

Claude didn't listen. With his free hand, he grabbed Christian's throat and took him to the ground. He subdued the younger male with a solid blow to the face.

Christian blinked up at him, dazed and confused about how quickly things had transpired.

Claude stared down at him, letting himself be washed over by the frustration and heat coursing through him.

Christian had betrayed him again.

With one knee on the small of Christian's back, pinning him, Claude took advantage of his slow-to-move state and ripped off his lover's pants with harsh jerks.

"Don't," Christian warned. He glanced over his shoulder at him, his gaze piercing. "Don't you fucking dare."

Claude gripped him by the back of his neck, forcing him face-first against the hard floor.

Christian groaned.

Rage seethed in the pit of Claude's stomach. "Don't I? It's all right for that bartender *friend* of yours to touch you, but I'm not allowed?"

"I didn't fuck Eric!"

"I've heard enough." Claude yanked down Christian's boxers, exposing his squirming, bare ass. At the sight, Claude's cock grew hard and heavy with the desire to claim Christian. He wasted no time undoing his own pants and pulling them down his thighs, baring his thick erection.

Though Christian fought to buck him off, his attempts were half-hearted at best. Either he was too inebriated, too high, or still stunned from Claude's blow. It didn't matter. Claude half straddled, half pinned him anyway. Hannah had once suggested he teach Christian a lesson for all the pain he'd caused, but Claude hadn't dared. The thought of making him unhappy, even a little, made his stomach churn.

Not anymore. He would make Christian pay for the betrayal, the lies, the stealing. All of it, he would dump into his body like waste.

Claude spit into the crack of Christian's ass.

Christian shuddered and mumbled incoherently.

Claude tuned him out. Not hesitating another moment longer, he worked his cock inside of his hot, tight hole.

A long, drawn-out cry escaped Christian, most likely due to the pain of being unprepared.

Claude groaned at the discomfort. Christian was unbearable. The position didn't help much, either. Claude had a quick moment to consider that if Christian had slept with Eric, he wouldn't be so tight. The realization wouldn't dissuade him, however. He could have easily taken Eric, and there was no accounting for the other times the two spent alone together.

Claude squeezed Christian's wrists above his head, more for balance than for subjugation. It took a great deal of work, but Claude finally burrowed himself as deep as possible, deep enough that they were almost one. They both groaned.

"Fuck," Christian cried out with a cracking voice.

Claude managed to find a rhythm. He held Christian down and pounded into his body with abandon, hammering into him all the pent-up pain and animosity he'd sheltered for years. For the past twelve months, Christian had been gone, left him without a single word. His cock might be chafed raw later, but it would be worth it.

"Please..." Christian begged in a low voice, so quiet Claude barely heard it. Christian lay unmoving beneath him, though his body was tense.

"Please what?" Claude groaned. He was close.

Christian didn't answer. Besides a whimper or two, his soft, labored panting filled the quiet space between them.

Claude eased his grip on Christian's wrists, allowing the younger male to prop up on his elbows. Christian did so, but otherwise made no move to leave. Claude smirked. "Should I make you come too?"

"Fuck you."

Claude frowned. Christian would never learn. He thrust into his ass harder and faster, ignoring his lover's cries, until his vision flickered and he ejaculated deep inside Christian's abused hole with an animalistic growl.

Christian shuddered beneath him as the tension melted away, leaving him a barely breathing puddle of mess.

Claude collapsed on him, overcome by a sudden sense of peace. Gone was the turmoil plaguing him for the last six hours. He'd shoved all of that into Christian, into his pores and his psyche, until it seeped from his soiled body onto the floor. As he placed a soft kiss on Christian's warm, pungent skin, guilt rode him hard and fast. Claude sat up, gaping at his lover's bruised and broken body, mortified that he could hurt Christian that way.

"What have I done?"

Christian glared back at him, his eyes red-rimmed with unshed tears, his lips set into a thin, harsh line that trembled. He didn't respond to Claude's question, yet the look was enough.

The damage was irreparable.

Chapter Nineteen

CLAUDE HAD APOLOGIZED and told Nick he was going into work. That had been hours earlier.

Hours before Nick was able to peel his sore body off the floor and limp to the bathroom. Shame filled him with every painful step he took. He couldn't remember the last time he'd felt so worthless. Was it the first time his own father molested him at eleven years old? Or maybe it was the first time he'd blown a guy for money eight years later. Nick couldn't say for sure. It'd been so long since then, the feeling was almost alien to him. Never did he ever think he'd go through that in his "home" with a man he called his boyfriend.

In the bathroom, Nick avoided looking at himself in the vanity mirror. He ran the hot water in the Jacuzzi bathtub and listlessly stripped off his shoes and what remained of his clothing. He'd have to replace the torn slacks.

Once the tub was filled, Nick sank into the scalding water with a wince. His ass was sore. Cum and blood seeped out of him while he soaked. Nick got comfortable, but he couldn't relax. His face throbbed from Claude's punch and his wrists were mottled a deep red from when Claude had held him while he'd...

Nick shook his head, refusing to go there. Refusing to say or even think that fucking word.

No denying he looked like a victim, but he couldn't see himself as such. He was a man, and men didn't get victimized. He could have *easily* fought Claude off. Could have made him regret ever touching him like that, but he'd wanted it.

Hell, he'd probably deserved it.

Nick remained in the tub until his skin resembled a giant prune. He bathed and dressed for work. Luckily, he kept a spare uniform. He met Frances outside half an hour later.

Frances stubbed out a cigarette when Nick joined him, although the smoky scent lingered on the cold air. The older man took one look at Nick's face, and he hesitated.

Nick instinctively cupped his own cheek. The skin was tender and a little puffy. He probably should have iced it before going into work.

He clenched his jaw, staring at Frances. "What?"

"Are you all right?"

"I'm fine. I didn't take you for the sympathetic type, though."

Frances pulled open the passenger door without a word. The compressed lips and soft eyes were replaced with his familiar hard mien.

Nick slumped into the seat, his lids heavy as lead. When was the last time he'd slept? His stomach growled. The last thing he'd eaten had been a second helping of chili at Eric's place nearly twelve hours back. Nick leaned his cheek against the cool window, wincing as it stung.

This was going to be a crappy-ass day.

BEING AT WORK, running on no sleep, little food, and too sore to move made Nick an irritable SOB.

That night happened to be a busy night, too. Usually, Nick handled high stress on the job well, but right then, he was a giant mess. He moved slowly, mixed up orders, forgot stuff, and was generally a pain in the ass to his boss, fellow employees, and customers too, based on the amount of tips he'd gotten so far.

Phil finally pulled him aside before he delivered two plates to one of his tables. "I got these, son. Why don't you take a break outside? Clear your head."

Nick wanted to protest, but he didn't. A break was the last thing he needed. He didn't want to spend time thinking about what had happened earlier.

Instead, he pulled off his apron and draped the fabric across his shoulders. "These go to table nine."

"They go to table seven," the chef yelled at him. Nick didn't miss the eye roll, either.

Phil shook his head. "I don't know what's wrong with you today, but go on and get your break."

Nick stormed outside, breathing in a mouthful of garbage-scented cold air. He walked behind the dark, empty alley, yearning to punch a hole through the brick wall. He itched with the need to light up and smoke until completely calm, but he'd probably lose his job.

"At least someone would like that," Nick mumbled. Claude would probably die of happiness if Nick were suddenly unemployed. Nick leaned against the side of the building and closed his eyes, even though he knew better than to let his guard down in a place like that. He didn't care. Pressed up against the wall, he could still feel Claude inside him, thick, hard, and angry.

When he'd gotten in that morning, he'd known there would be an argument. Afterward, however, he'd anticipated a nice, hard fucking to end the animosity, and pancakes to make up for it. Then he'd go to work and things would be cool between them.

He hadn't expected what *actually* happened that morning. Nick had been so stunned, he hadn't been able to properly defend himself. He'd reverted back to his kid self, scared and pissed-off. Teary eyed. Helpless.

"Hey."

Nick's eyes shot open. He glanced at his best friend's dark silhouette several feet away from him. Nick pushed off the wall and grounded himself in reality. "Hey."

Eric closed the distance between them, his hands shoved into his coat pockets for warmth. "You okay?"

"Yeah."

"I see you in there, man. You're off tonight." Eric hesitated, licking his lips. "Is this because of last night? I'm so sorry, I didn't mean to kiss you. We were drinking. Smoking. I got caught up in the moment."

Nick shook his head, chuckling softly at the worry in Eric's tone. "No, it's fine. We're cool."

Tension left Eric's shoulders.

"I was actually gonna ask if it's okay if I stay at your place for a little while. Just until I find a new apartment."

Eric nodded. "You don't even got to ask, *hermano*. You and your boy...you get into it?"

"Something like that."

"One more thing, yo. I've been meaning to ask all night. What the fuck happened to your face?"

Nick hesitated. He really didn't want to tell Eric that his lover had nearly KO'd him, though to be fair, he'd thrown the first punch. The first several of them. "Fucking fell," he mumbled. It sounded lame as hell even to himself.

Eric scoffed. "Don't give me that bullshit. He hit you, didn't he?"

Nick looked down at the dirty slush beneath his shoes.

"Did he?" Eric demanded. "That motherfucking, *gringo pendejo* punched you in the fucking face."

Nick sighed. "We got into a fight, okay? And yeah, he hit me in the face. Big fucking deal. I've had worse."

"Fuck, man." Eric paced the small space. "You want me to whip his ass, yo? 'Cause I'll fucking do it. I don't give a shit. That abusive crap don't ride with me."

"It don't fucking ride with me, either," Nick said, offended at the implication that he let it happen. Even if it really was the cold hard truth. He exhaled a deep breath, trying to calm himself. That was not the time or place to be rallying his boys to dish out revenge. "Just come with me to the penthouse after work so I can get my stuff, okay?"

Eric nodded. "Okay." He wrapped one arm around Nick's shoulder, pulling him against his thick body for a tight hug. "I'm glad you're coming home with me, Nicky. I always said you belong with me. That *pinche puta* don't deserve you, man."

Nick snorted. He was the one who didn't deserve good, not with the kind of life he'd led up until then. He patted Eric's back and pretended to agree with him. "Yeah, man. I'm glad I'm coming home with you too."

Chapter Twenty

PHIL RELEASED NICK from work earlier than usual with the message to take the night off to get his shit together. Eric asked to be let off early so he could "take care of him." Phil had agreed. Nick wanted to be offended, but he really did need Eric.

Eric drove his friend's car to the tower Claude called home. He parked out front. "Need me to come inside?"

Nick shook his head. "I won't be long." If he left behind most of the crap Claude had bought for him since they'd been together, Nick would be done in a few minutes.

It was close to midnight. Nick used his key to take the elevator to Claude's floor. His heart hammered as he ascended. What if Claude was up? What if he was pissed off again? Nick shook his head, clearing his mind of the useless thoughts. He wasn't afraid of Claude.

The elevator to his suite opened, instantly greeting him with the aroma of Creole seasonings, tomatoes, green peppers, and some kind of marinara sauce. Though the penthouse was dark, there wasn't that same ominous presence like there'd been earlier. Candles were lit everywhere, giving the place an ambient glow. A trumpet played a soft tune in the background. Chris Botti. Claude loved the guy's music.

"You're home early." Claude padded into the living room with bare feet and scotch in hand, dressed casually in monogrammed sweatpants and a form-fitting T-shirt. His hair was slightly damp, plastered around his handsome, dewy face. He'd just gotten out of the shower. "Dinner's not quite ready, but it will be shortly. Why don't you sit down and have a drink? I'll take your coat."

Nick stepped back, out of his reach. He swallowed hard while staring into Claude's puzzled features. "I'm not staying for dinner."

"I have a gift for you." Claude sauntered off into the bedroom, leaving Nick standing there with no fucking clue what to do.

Nick raked his cold hands over his face. He pulled off his hood and removed his hat. The room had gotten stuffy all of a sudden.

Claude returned with a hard case. "Open it."

Nick eyed the expensive-looking case, making no moves to reach for it. "What is it?" He had a feeling he knew the answer.

Claude gladly opened the box, revealing a stunning watch with a brown dial and pink-gold hour-markers and hands. The strap appeared to be hand-stitched brown alligator. "This is a Jules Audemars self-winding watch. It indicates the day, the date, the moon phases, the month, and the leap years. There are at least thirty-eight jewels inside." Claude pointed the case in his direction. "The casing alone is made of 18-carat pink gold and glare-proof sapphire crystal. It's all yours."

Nick frowned. He didn't want to imagine how much Claude had paid for the watch. Even in the dim candlelight, it shone. He cleared his throat, wanting to get back to the real reason why he'd come back.

"I'm leaving for a little while."

Claude's face fell. His smile just dropped away, melting into a frown like it was the most natural thing. "What?"

Nick walked past him, headed for the bedroom. "I'm here to get my stuff." He didn't want any complications.

Claude gripped his shoulder, spinning him around. "Christian—"

Nick shoved him away. He balled his fists at his side, his jaw tense as white-hot fury flared through him. "For the last time, that isn't my name. I'm Nick, for fuck's sake." He took several deep breaths, reining in the rage threatening to spill all over Claude for continuing to mistake him for his ex-lover. Even though he'd corrected him numerous times. "What happened to Christian, anyway?"

Claude's eyes widened. "What?"

"The real Christian didn't just up and leave you. His family reported him as a missing person almost a year ago. Know what I think? Something happened to Christian, and I think you know exactly what that is."

Claude's features darkened, his eyes appearing black in the poor lighting. "What are you talking about?" he asked in a low voice. "Stop speaking nonsense."

"Whatever, I'm done. I'm leaving." He stood in Claude's personal space, so close that the spicy oak scent of Claude's breath fell against his cheek. They were close enough to kiss. The heat from Claude's body nearly singed him, chasing away whatever cold had seeped through him since coming in from outside. "And you're not gonna stop me."

He waited for Claude to retaliate. To get mad and try to pin him down again. Claude didn't. He took two steps back, his careful gaze still on Nick, and then finally he disappeared into the kitchen.

Nick turned away, barely able to breathe past the thick tension. He hurried to the bedroom and snatched his overnight bag, stuffing it with his old clothing and shoes. He shoved his laptop beneath his arm and headed for the elevator again.

He reached for the button to call the thing up, but stopped before his finger made contact. He glanced over his shoulder, in the direction of the kitchen where Claude had gone. Not a peep came from that area. Claude didn't come out and try to stop him, either.

Nick shook his head of any delusions and pressed the button. What the hell was he hoping for?

Bitterness rode him hard as he made his way outside to Eric's friend's parked car. Even twenty feet away, the loud Latin hip-hop blasted from the speakers. Eric was probably doing it to piss off the residents. Nick pulled open the back door and set his stuff inside.

"Yo, you got a couple dollars on you? I need to gas this baby before we go home."

"Yeah, hold on." Nick retrieved his wallet and reached inside for whatever cash he had on him. Instead, his fingers found something small, paper-y, and cylindrical. Frowning, he pulled the object out.

It was one of Claude's Turkish cigarettes. The one he'd taken the first night he'd met the guy. The paper was all crinkly and banged up, but the dark, exotic scent still lingered as he put the thing to his nose. Memories of Claude filled him. Happier ones.

Nick tossed the thing onto the ground and stomped on it, smashing the cigarette into the melted snow. He slid into the passenger seat, refusing to look up at the skyscraper building.

"Let's go."

Chapter Twenty-One

CLAUDE SAT AT the dining room table, staring at nothing he could discern with his current frame of mind. He held the half-empty glass like a lifeline, clenching and unclenching his fist around it. The scent of his blackened tilapia filled the air, tainted by a burnt undertone. The spaghetti squash marinara also smelled overdone. He knew he needed to turn the stove off. He also needed to blow out the candles lest they melt all over his furnishings and become impossible to clean. Yet for some reason, he couldn't move. His body remained glued to the seat, images of Christian filling his mind. Images of the time they'd spent together recently. As Claude mechanically raised the glass to his lips, the memories faded away, replaced by the vivid scene of pale blue eyes, bulging with fear and filled with blood.

Claude hissed at the sudden stab to his temples. He dropped the cup in favor of massaging his skull. Just as quickly as it'd appeared, the scene vanished, leaving behind no sense of comprehension. Claude shook his head, smacked his cheek until it stung, but still he couldn't erase what he'd seen. His breathing rate quickened as guilt consumed him.

What if "Nick" is right? What if he really isn't Christian? What if the real Christian is gone for good?

"No," Claude croaked. "God, no."

He didn't want to imagine it. Couldn't bear the thought of Christian being gone from his life.

Sweat dotted his forehead, and Claude swiped at it. His body grew rigid. He sucked in a deep breath as his cock throbbed. He ached all over, like an addict in withdrawal, craving his favorite drug.

He needed Christian. And no matter what, he would never let Christian go.

NICK DIDN'T SLEEP well.

All night, he tossed and turned on Eric's couch, his mind stuck on Claude. From the beginning, he'd known the entire thing would be a mistake. Not only because they'd moved too quickly, either. Something had been off about Claude. He'd called him by another guy's name, and even shot his pursuer in the leg with no hesitation. What normal man does that?

Nick fluffed the pillow beneath his head and stared up at the ceiling, unable to discern anything. He trailed his hand down his chest, coming to rest below his navel. He missed sleeping in Claude's king-size bed, tangled up in silk sheets and limbs.

No one had ever touched him the way Claude did. Over the last month, he'd gotten used to Claude's snug, large hands skimming across his body; his smooth lips and skilled tongue kissing him in places he didn't even know could feel good. And his cock...

Jesus, the man was hung and he knew how to use it, too.

Nick sucked in a deep breath and rearranged his pajama bottoms. In the quiet dark, with only the occasional police siren blaring by, Nick was lonely as fuck. He closed his eyes, trying to remember the last time they'd made love. All he kept getting was yesterday morning, remembering the strength of Claude's viselike grip on his wrists, and the weight of his body pressing him against the cold hard floor while he fucked him raw.

Nick's dick swelled. His upper lip curled in disgust at the arousing thought. Closing his eyes, Nick cleared his mind of everything and forced himself to sleep.

"Nicky. Wake up, bro."

Nick cracked open his lids to Eric's deep accented voice, and the smell of something buttery and sweet.

Eric held out a paper bag from the corner bodega. "I got breakfast."

Nick peered around the living room, illuminated by the sun's rays. He stretched and groaned. "What time is it?"

"Nine o'clock. Move over." Eric shoved his legs aside so he could sit on the couch. He spread out his bacon, egg, and cheese sandwich and lit up.

"Thanks."

Eric blew a cloud of thick smoke away from him. "How'd you sleep?"

"Like shit. And that's not only because you have a crappy-ass couch, either." He forced himself to grin at his best friend.

"Damn, you got jokes. That's cool."

Nick unraveled his own breakfast and bit into the soft lukewarm sandwich before popping open his can of Arizona tea.

"Make sure you eat up, man. I wanna go jogging after we eat. It'll be good for you."

Nick snorted. "I don't see how you do it. Jogging in the city."

"You got a problem with jogging, bro?"

"Here I do." The entire city stunk to high heaven of piss, wet garbage, fish slime, and God only knows what else. It wasn't too bad in the winter, though nothing could ever make the horrible smell go away. "I'd pass out after a half mile. Not because of the cold air filling my lungs, either."

Eric tsked at him. "Pussy. We'll do the gym, then. Is that cool, *Su Alteza*?"

Nick nodded. He hadn't gotten a good workout in too long.

Eric fired up the PlayStation, and they ate in silence. Nick couldn't focus on the video game images. He poked at the remainder of his BEC until the thing resembled mincemeat. His chest was heavy.

"You okay, *hermano?*"

Nick shook his head, avoiding his friend's dark gaze. "I don't want to lose him, Eric."

Silence. "What are you trying to say?" Eric finally asked.

Nick closed his eyes, wishing he could shut himself off from the world. "I don't know, but I have some kind of feelings for him."

"Are you insane, *vato?*"

Eric's sharp tone cut through his silent mood, forcing his lids open. He focused on his best friend's frowning face. "Maybe I am."

"You must fucking be if you're talking about having feelings for him. *Él es un perro loco, ése.*"

"You don't think I know that?"

"You must don't." Eric stood then, stabbing out his joint in the copper ashtray on the coffee table. "The guy don't even see you, man. He looks at you, and he sees his ex. He's fucking you, but his mind is thinking about that other dude."

Nick stared at him, his mouth taut. The food he'd just eaten left a bitter taste on his tongue. "Enough."

Eric's features softened. "I'm just saying—"

"Fuck you."

Nick pushed the blanket off his lap and headed for the bathroom. He needed to get showered and dressed. Fuck the gym, he needed to see Amy.

"Where you going?"

"Hospital."

"I'll come with you."

Nick glared at his friend over his shoulder. A part of him didn't want to be around the bastard, even though Eric only pointed out the truth—something a concerned friend would do if he actually gave a damn.

"Fine."

It was still cold and early by the time they reached the New York Med. Nick hadn't talked to Eric during the trip. And Eric hadn't said anything, either. He'd remained firm in his stance, pissed at Nick's revelation.

As if Nick could control his feelings.

They walked down the familiar hallway in silence, nodded at familiar faces before they reached Amy's room. Nick tapped twice on her door, not wanting to startle her. She'd had more treatment last night, so she was probably resting.

"Come in," Amy's cheerful voice called from the other side.

Nick smiled as he stepped inside. She seemed to be in a good mood.

Amy sat up in bed, a ton of manga and anime magazines sprawled across her blanket-covered lap. She beamed at him with no tiredness on her face, just a radiant smile.

Sitting next to her, dressed to kill in a designer pin-stripe suit and understated jewelry, was Claude.

Nick met his stony gaze with a frown.

"Nick, look who came to see me," Amy said. She held up a handful of Japanese comics with sparkly big-eyed girls on the covers. "And look what he bought me!"

Nick opened his mouth to speak, then closed it. He was speechless.

"What the *hell* are you doing here?" Eric asked from behind him. Nick turned around to note his best friend glowering at Claude, brow furrowed and teeth bared like a dog about to attack.

Claude stood. He didn't so much as glance Eric's way. His eyes were all for Nick. "I need to talk to you."

"How'd you know I would be here?"

Claude gave him a small smile. "I know you too well...Nick."

Nick's heart dropped into his stomach. Claude had never called him by his actual name. He focused his gaze on the older man, who remained stoic, though Nick noted the pleading behind his gaze.

"Let's go outside."

"Go outside?" Eric remarked with disbelief evident in his voice. "You really gonna listen to what this fool has to say, Nick? He's crazy. He fucking hit you, for chrissakes, and you wanna talk to him?"

Amy gaped at Claude's back. "You *hit* my brother?"

Claude turned toward her. Though Nick couldn't catch his expression, he was sure Claude wore a reassuring smile.

"It was a misunderstanding," Claude explained.

"Misunderstanding, my ass, *pendejo*. I'll show you a misunderstanding."

"Eric," Nick shouted. "That's enough. Not in front of Amy."

Eric shook his head, his gaze filled with confusion. "Are you serious, bro? After everything he—"

"If you don't like it, you can leave."

Eric threw his hands up. He took a step backward. "All right, Nick. Whatever you want, man." He pulled open the door and left.

Nick sighed. He'd gone there to see his sister, not deal with that shit. He stared at Claude, knowing he needed to at least get that out of the way if he hoped to enjoy his visit with her.

Nick walked past Claude to stand at Amy's bedside. He leaned in close, placing a kiss on her smooth forehead. "I'll be right back, okay?"

Amy nodded, the worried expression still there. "Is everything okay?"

"Everything's fine, Aims." He gave her a tight squeeze before heading for the door. Nick stepped outside, expecting Claude to follow.

He did.

As Claude closed the door behind him, Nick tried desperately to hold onto the anger that burned deep inside him for the man, but staring at him in his tailored suit, wool trench coat, and leather gloves, with his dark-blond locks so effortlessly neat, all he could think about was how amazing he looked. And smelled. The sensual scent of earth, wood, and spices, with a hint of grapefruit and geranium, overpowered the antiseptic smell, reminding him of times he spent beneath his powerful body. Nick licked his lips. Maybe being alone with him was a bad idea.

"Don't ever come here to see Amy without me, understand?" Nick warned.

Claude nodded.

"What do you want?"

Claude's hand disappeared into his coat. A moment later, he retrieved a dark-ruby velvet case big enough for a ring. "One more chance."

Nick looked fixedly at the box, his heart hammering.

"I'm so sorry." Claude took a deep, shuddering breath and closed the distance between them. "I promise I'll do everything within my power to make it up to you." He wrapped his arms around Nick's shoulders and slumped against him.

Nick couldn't bring himself to move.

"Please...give me one more chance. Please don't leave me again."

Nick placed his hands on Claude's sides. Instead of hugging him, however, he pushed them apart. The sadness in Claude's gaze made his stomach churn. "I can't. I mean, I need some time, Claude." Despite his feelings, returning to the relationship wasn't such a good idea. Claude was unstable. Nick wasn't sure how long that would last, either. Even if he did go back, things would probably never be the way they were in the beginning. Nick twisted around to head back into Amy's room.

"So that's it?"

He glanced over his shoulder in time to notice Claude's frown. "What?"

"You're going to leave me and go home with Eric, despite everything I've done for you?"

Nick calmly shook his head. He didn't want to argue. "Time, Claude. I need time." *And space.*

Claude wasn't deterred. "I took care of you when no one else would. Where was Eric when your apartment was broken into? Where was Eric when that thug tried to attack you in the streets?" Claude's features darkened, and he said in a low voice, "I killed that man for you. Can Eric say he's done the same?"

Nick gave him wide eyes, stunned by his words, spoken with seriousness. "You need to leave."

"Christian—"

"Now." Nick rushed into Amy's room and shut the door behind him, his hand glued to the knob in case Claude attempted to follow him inside. His palms were sweaty despite the cool temperature inside the hospital.

"Nick..."

Nick spun around to face Amy's worried mien. His chest ached, and he exhaled, not realizing he'd been holding his breath. "Yeah?"

"Are you okay?"

"Yeah. Why?"

"You're death-gripping the door."

Nick gazed down at his mottled hand and finally let go. He approached Amy's bedside and occupied Claude's former seat. The chair still smelled like his favorite cologne. "What did Claude want? He didn't say anything weird to you, did he?"

Amy shook her head. "No, he literally came to see how I was doing. He asked about my treatments and talked to Dr. Thompson about making sure I had the best of the best. Something like that." Amy shrugged. "That was it."

"Oh." Nick relaxed a degree. Of course the guy wanted to check on her, given he was paying for all her medical expenses.

"I forgot one other thing."

Nick perked up. "What?"

"It was so weird, actually. A man came into my room and handed me an envelope. Then he left without a word."

Nick's heart stopped. "What?"

Amy scrolled through a magazine as if bored of the conversation. "Yeah, Claude took it before I could see what was in it."

"What did this man look like, Aims?"

She stared at the ceiling, furrow between her brows, concentrating. "Short. Mohawk. Dark, small eyes. I think he was Mexican. He had a lot of tattoos from what I could make out."

Nick slumped into his seat, his gaze distant as he searched his memory for a person like that from his past. There were none. But the guy coming to see his sister wasn't a coincidence. Nick thought back to the night his place was broken into. To his sister's defiled image, with the word SLUT written beneath her face.

"Oh, God," he whispered.

Chapter Twenty-Two

CLAUDE SIPPED HIS wine and stared across the room with disdain. Eric Ruiz stood behind the ebony wood bar, conversing with a customer, though he couldn't make out his words over the local jazz band playing onstage.

Claude didn't need to know what he was saying. He was there for one purpose only.

His watch read ten o'clock when Eric asked a coworker to cover for him. He disappeared inside the double doors leading into the back.

Claude got to his feet. He knew exactly where Eric was going.

Claude withdrew outside, buttoning his coat as he went. The foul scent of rotten garbage tickled his nose as he stalked into the alleyway. The click of a lighter sounded nearby, followed by a soft inhale then exhale. The first tinges of tobacco floated in the air.

Eric didn't move from his spot against the filthy brick wall once Claude approached. He blew another cloud of smoke and smirked at him. "You been watching me all night. Something you wanna ask me, gringo?"

Claude reached into his inside coat pocket, retrieving the small white envelope he'd taken from Amy yesterday. He tossed it into the frozen slush at Eric's feet. "I know you had something to do with this."

Eric hesitated a moment before he picked it up. Cigarette held firmly between his lips, he opened the envelope to examine its contents. Inside was a picture of Amy, taken unsuspectingly at the hospital. Her eyes were blacked out with a marker. Beneath her face, the words "Dead Slut" had been scribbled.

Eric's features twisted in pain, briefly, before returning to a stoic façade. "What the hell makes you think I'd do something like this?"

"I don't trust you."

"I don't give a shit whether you trust me or not, ése. Amy is my hermanita. My baby sister. I'd kill the bastard who did this."

Claude deliberately shook his head, his gaze raking over the bartender with contempt. Ruiz seemed like a man after something. Whether that was just Christian or something more, Claude wasn't entirely sure.

What he was certain of was that he didn't want him near Christian anymore.

Claude closed the distance between them until they were chest to chest.

Eric moved from his slumped position, standing straight as a rod at his full height. His features were tight, indignation palpable beneath the surface.

"I don't know what you want, but I'm advising you to stay away from him. For your own sake."

Eric gave him a lopsided grin. "Him who? You mean Nick? Or Christian?"

Claude growled low at his mocking smile.

Eric didn't relent. "You don't even see him, yo. You're too busy chasing the past and not even realizing what you got right in front of you. I'd be better for him anyway. You're just a delusional psycho, cabrón."

Claude shoved him against the wall.

Eric's jaw dropped a moment before he threw his fist at Claude's head. Much like he'd done with Christian, Claude caught Ruiz's arm and used his leverage to drag him onto the ground.

Before the fiery Hispanic attacked, Claude pinned his arms down with his knees and set his weight on Eric's upper back.

"Get the fuck up off me, cabrón," Eric snarled.

Claude's upper lip curled in revulsion at the cold, dirty ice seeping into the knees of his tailored pants. He hadn't expected their conversation to get that out of hand. He couldn't imagine how much worse Eric must feel, pressed face-first into the piss-ridden snow. He wasn't wearing a coat even, obviously having no plans to stay out there that long.

Something scurrying away from the dumpster caught Claude's attention. Most likely a rat. As he redirected his attention toward Eric—still swearing at him in Spanish—something dark caught his eye. Something beneath Eric's shirt.

Claude frowned. A small inconspicuous tattoo rested on Eric's lower back. Claude raised the shirt higher to get a better look.

"What the fuck are you doing?" Eric's voice held the slightest tang of fear.

Claude ignored him as he bent down to examine the words clearly. The lighting in the area was terrible. A criminal could easily relegate himself to darkness and attempt whatever he wanted there.

Eric bucked beneath him like a wild stallion trying to get free. Claude held firmly. The tattoo was intricately done, though placed a bit more to the side than directly on the lower back. Black cursive lettering read: Los Gorillas.

Claude scowled. He had no clue what that meant. There were more surrounding tattoos, making it harder to notice. A light bulb went off in his head, then. The man who'd sent the envelope wore L and G tattooed on his index and pinky fingers. Could LG stand for Los Gorillas?

Was it a coincidence? *I think not.*

Claude finally let Eric go. His face mottled, Eric jumped up, his entire uniform wet with frozen bits of slush sticking to him. "You're gonna pay for that. I swear to God you're gonna pay."

Claude ignored his threat. "I'm assuming Los Gorillas is the name of a gang. Is Christian aware of your lowlife affiliation?" He couldn't imagine Christian wanting to stay around a man of that caliber.

"*Nick* knows all about my past. There's no secrets between us. Hell, besides, he used to be in a gang too."

Claude's body stiffened, his hard gaze locked on Eric's smug face. "Liar." His voice was barely more than a growl.

"Oh, what, you didn't know? Nah, yeah, little Nicky ain't the innocent you thought he was. Being tangled up in gangs is how me and him got so tight in the first place. But we ain't involved in that stuff no more. I mean, if we were, would we be working for minimum wage and shitty tips in a bar?"

Claude shook his head, uncaring about anything other than the revelation Eric just laid bare. The mystery of what Christian had been involved in had been solved. It was likely Eric could be lying, but why else would Christian be around him?

"Stay away from him. This is the only warning you'll get from me."

"Or else what?"

Claude glared at the younger male, allowing him to witness the rage clouding his features. He turned away without a single word.

Chapter Twenty-Three

NICK SHOVED HIS yet-to-be-returned key into the lock that would get the elevator working. Standing alone beneath fluorescent lights, Nick stared at his reflection through the steel. His body wired, teeth bared, and brows furrowed, he looked like a madman.

This is the final straw.

He was done with Claude.

When the doors finally opened, Nick stormed into the darkened penthouse, the only light filling the area coming from the kitchen.

Claude sat on the living room sofa, deep in thought, hands folded in his lap while he stared at nothing. He didn't so much as glance Nick's way.

What the hell was wrong with him? "Claude."

Claude glanced up. Though too dark to tell, he seemed surprised to find Nick standing there. "Christian?" Claude sighed with relief. "I knew you'd be back. Care for something to drink?"

"You attacked Eric," Nick stated.

Claude stood. "Yes." As he approached him, Nick hit the switch, bathing the room in light. Claude shielded his eyes. How long had he been sitting in the dark? Claude sported an unkempt five o'clock shadow, something Nick had never seen on the guy. Even his clothes, nice as they were, looked rumpled and thrown on. After his eyes adjusted to the light, Claude beamed at Nick, his gaze shining with love.

Nick recoiled. Claude actually thought he'd come back to stay. "You attacked Eric," he repeated, "outside of work. For no reason. Have you lost your fucking mind? What is your problem?"

Claude didn't answer. He observed Nick as if trying to guess how he should go about dealing with that conversation.

"Amy told me about the envelope. Give it to me."

Claude retrieved the white envelope from his coat pocket; his favorite Hugo Boss coat that was just tossed onto the arm of the sofa, not hung up in the closet. He appeared hesitant, but finally he handed it to him.

Nick opened the thing and pulled out the single small picture. His hands trembled as he focused on it. Tears pricked the backs of his eyes while bile boiled hot in the pit of his gut. He opened his mouth to speak, yell, cry, or cuss. Only a choked sob escaped him.

"The man who delivered that envelope to the hospital had the letters L and G tattooed onto his fingers. Eric has a tattoo across his lower back that reads Los Gorillas, a street gang he used to be affiliated with."

Nick gawked at him with disbelief. "What?" he asked, his voice cracking.

"He told me himself. The reason you two are so close is because you both were in a gang." Claude glared at him with bright pin-point pupils. "Is this true?"

Nick shuffled to the couch on leaden feet, taking a seat on the arm before he fell over. He didn't see anything, though his eyes were wide open. He couldn't even tell what he was looking at.

"No," he whispered. It was partially true, however.

"I should have known he was lying."

Claude wandered off somewhere, but Nick didn't pay attention. He clasped his hands in his lap, head bowed with disbelief. Eric had been in a gang? How could that have escaped Nick, all the years they'd been friends? Of course, Nick had his suspicions. The way Eric acted sometimes seemed straight out of a manual for Latino gangsters. Nick assumed the guy was a poser. A wannabe thug. After all, he worked in a bar, got along with everyone, and never got into fights. Nick raked a hand through his hair, wanting to pull the shit out by the roots. If he'd known Eric had once been involved with a gang, no way Nick would have ever befriended him. Not after his own past with gangs.

Claude set a glass of amber liquid in front of him. "It's scotch."

Nick brought the drink to his lips, inhaling the aromatic scent of warm oak and spices while the rich, smoky taste slid down his throat. He emptied it.

Claude refilled his glass. "I know you're not the person Eric says you are. Why would you, of all people, involve yourself with the likes of street rats?"

Nick finished his second round. "I need to go see him." He didn't understand why Eric never told him about Los Gorillas, but he planned on finding out. He crumpled the picture of Amy in his fist. He would also find out who the hell was threatening him and his sister, and put a stop to it. Nick headed for the elevator, but Claude blocked his way. Nick glared at him. "Move."

Claude refused to budge. "That man is a dangerous criminal. Are you seriously planning on going back to him?"

Nick nodded. Unlike Claude as of late, he actually felt safe around Eric. If the guy had been in a gang, Nick only wanted to know why. Maybe he'd had no choice, similar to what Nick had gone through.

"Will you just fucking move? I really don't have the time or the energy to deal with you right now."

"I apologize for that." He placed his hands on Nick's shoulders, his gaze lingering on Nick's lips, eyes filled with longing. "Stay with me tonight." Claude leaned in close, pressing his lips to Nick's neck.

Nick's breath caught in his throat, surrounded by Claude's heat and familiar scent. He remained glued to the spot, shuddering as Claude's tongue swept across his Adam's apple.

Claude continued in a low, deep voice, his accent more prominent. "Let me make it up to you, please, *mijn lief.*"

Nick gripped Claude's shoulders. He squeezed his eyes shut as Claude's scorching wet lips found his. God, he wanted to... It would be easier to give in and let things work out from there. Yet despite the searing kiss, his body remained tense, as if the thought of Claude inside him repulsed it.

Claude moved in to suck his tongue, but Nick pushed him away with the force of a gnat. He was tired. The whole situation was draining.

Taking hold of Claude's hand, Nick dropped the key into his palm. "You and me? I don't think we should see each other anymore."

Claude gazed at his hand, then back at Nick. His face was so stoic, it was impossible to guess what the man's thoughts were. Goose bumps covered Nick's arms, even though they were in the warmth of Claude's penthouse.

"Well, goodbye then." Nick spun around and headed for the elevator before he changed his mind. He pushed his finger on the Down button. Spots filled his vision, suddenly, and his body slumped forward like deadweight. Stunned, Nick turned toward Claude, but his vision left and so did his consciousness.

CLAUDE STROKED CHRISTIAN'S hair. He couldn't fathom why he found it so damn difficult to tear his gaze away from Christian's face—scrunched up as if in pain, even in deep sleep. Claude stretched his tired arms to the sides. He'd been watching Christian sleep for the last six hours.

Sunlight streamed in through the windows, followed by the condensation of a cold spring morning in New York. Claude sipped his Jamaican coffee. Questions raced through his mind in a perpetual loop. Who was Nick? Had Christian lied about his identity to him the entire time? Why had a gang member chased him into the streets? Many more filled his head until Claude could no longer decipher the blur of words.

The soft sound of Christian stirring brought Claude's attention to the younger male. Hard metal clanking against marble sent a shock down his spine.

Christian pried open his eyes and blinked up at Claude.

"Good morning, Christian."

Christian's green gaze flared across the room. His compressed lips shifted downward. "Why are we in the bathroom?" Abruptly, he stood, and that time, the sound of metal hitting porcelain appeared to be a wake-up smack to the face. Christian finally took notice of the chain, one end attached to the back of the toilet. The other was firmly locked into a dog collar, wrapped tight around Christian's neck.

"What the fuck?" Christian whispered, eyes wide and filled with disbelief.

"Vicky made your favorite breakfast again. I'll heat it up for you."

"What the fuck did you do?" Christian shouted.

Claude twisted his expression as pain pierced his heart. He'd never meant to do that to him. "I'm keeping you safe."

"You psychotic bastard." Christian struggled with the chain, attempting with all his strength to break it. He gritted his teeth, pulled, and strained until veins bulged through his lean muscles.

Claude merely observed him. "I'll release you once you've answered my questions. Tell me honestly, and you won't ever have to worry about me anymore." Claude swallowed past the tightness in his throat. It hurt him to think Christian would never speak to him again. "Is that understood?"

"Fuck you! I hope you rot in hell, you piece of shit."

Claude left the master bathroom. Time. Christian needed a little time to calm down from the shock of his situation. Claude withdrew into the kitchen and grabbed the plastic-wrapped plate Vicky had left behind for Christian. He shoved it into the microwave on high, filling the space with the scent of eggs, bacon, and blueberry pancakes. Once it was thoroughly warm, Claude poured a glass of freshly squeezed orange juice and returned to the master bathroom.

Christian's shrill cry for help pierced Claude's eardrums.

Claude pushed open the door, setting the plate and cup onto the marble countertop. He strode toward Christian, shutting him up with a hand over his mouth. "No one can hear you. I hope you know that. I have the entire floor to myself. The walls are soundproof."

Christian glowered at him, the heat of his skin practically singeing Claude's palm.

Claude let go. "What have you been doing since you left me twelve months ago?"

"Fuck you."

Claude closed his eyes and took a deep breath. When he reopened them, Christian still beheld him with hatred flaming in his gaze. Christian tugged at the collar around his neck so hard, Claude was sure he'd acquire bruises. Still, the metal contraption would not come off, no matter how much he struggled. The piece remained firmly clamped until Claude unlocked it.

Claude stood. "I'm going to work now. Try to eat your breakfast." He exited the bathroom without a backward glance. Work was the last thing he wanted to do, but Claude dressed and rang Frances anyway. He peered up at the twentieth floor from outside, hating to leave Christian alone, yet knowing it was necessary. Perhaps Christian would be more compliant by the time he returned.

Claude shook with anxiety once they reached his father's company. Dread filled him. A long day of meetings, checking the books, and inventory awaited. Claude slid on his D&G aviators and dragged himself into work. The lobby was busier than normal. Employees bustled about, scurrying off to do whatever they did every day in that place. The company had received double the orders for luxury yachts, almost twice more than their most successful quarter during his father's time as CEO. Claude ambled through, ignoring several greetings on the way to his office. His mind still cloudy, he possessed no clue how he would get a single thing done that day.

"Mr. Vanderpoel."

Claude gave pause at the familiar feminine voice. He turned to find Hannah trotting up to his side. She wore a professional smile, but her brown eyes gleamed with mischief.

Claude inclined his head to her. "Hannah."

"Good morning, sir. I see you've gone for a new look." She placed a manicured finger to her chin. "I'm not sure I like the rugged look on you, yet."

Claude took in his attire. Not only had he not shaved his two-day beard or properly combed his hair, he'd put on black leather pants—the only pair he owned—and paired it with a T-shirt, boots, and a denim jacket. The jacket had been a gift from his mother several years back. He actually despised denim.

"These are going to the Goodwill store on 72nd Street, actually." They'd been set out just for that purpose.

Hannah gave him a knowing smirk. "Of course. So, how are things with Nick?"

"Excuse me?"

Hannah flinched, though Claude wasn't aware of his current expression. "Christian?"

Claude thought about the young male, chained up in his bathroom. Had he even touched his food? Did he hate him? "What do you have for me today?"

Hannah's expression morphed into the businesswoman façade she usually kept reserved for clients or around other employees.

iPad in the crook of her arm, she scrolled through her notes. "The investors confirmed they will be at the Millennium Broadway New York today for the three o'clock meeting."

Claude paused with his hand on the sleek knob of his office door. He frowned. "I'm meeting with the investors today?"

Hannah mirrored his expression. "Yes, sir. You had me send out emails last month." She pulled up her company email account. "On the thirteenth."

Claude exhaled a deep breath. Just one day before Christian had returned to his life. No wonder he'd forgotten. "Reschedule the meeting."

Hannah gaped at him, horrified, her rouged lips parted far apart. "I don't think that's a good idea, sir."

"Check my schedule for next month. I'd prefer a date around the end of it, if possible."

Hannah leaned in close to whisper, in a harsh voice, "Are you out of your goddamned mind, Claude? Do you know how busy our investors are? How far they traveled? Mrs. Studemayer cut her trip in Ibiza short to be here for this."

Claude's jaw tightened at the first stirrings of anger coursing through him. "You will do as I ask, Hannah, if you wish to keep your job."

"You know that if I cancel the company's most important annual meeting, your father will kill us both."

"I'm not afraid of my father."

"But *I* am."

Claude stared at her for a moment, noting the slightly widened eyes and clenching hands.

He pulled open the door and shut himself inside alone. Hannah's silhouette lingered at the door for several heartbeats before she finally left to complete her own work for the day. Claude sat at his desk and powered on his laptop. Once he got to the home screen, he searched through his files until he found the necessary document. The one for the annual investors' meeting. Claude skimmed through what was essentially a detailed list of the company's objectives for the future. The company's progress and growth in the past five years. Also, financial projections for the coming fiscal year, because that was the most important thing: how much richer could he make them.

There were other minutiae, such as expansion possibilities and the technological advancements for future watercraft—how he would continue to make Vanderpoel yachts faster, safer, and more functional than the competition.

All of it was no more than pretty talk and projections. Hopes and dreams he sold in a bottle to the investors to drink up and keep their money pooled into Vanderpoel's massive bank account. The actual growth of the business never went as planned. The numbers on the report were supposed to look good, to assure the investors that their money was in capable hands.

Meanwhile, Claude worked his ass off trying to reach those impossible numbers, and each year, his efforts went unappreciated by the man who mattered the most.

His resolve set in stone, Claude printed out the ten-page document and placed them into a crisp manila envelope. He paged his assistant. "Ms. Aldridge, step into my office, please."

Hannah appeared barely a minute later. "You called for me, sir?" She met his gaze directly, her face stern, mouth tense.

Claude slid the folder across the desk. "Take it."

Hannah hesitated before she picked it up. "What is it?"

"The document for the meeting with the investors. I typed it up some time ago."

Hannah tilted her head with uncertainty, her blonde hair spilling past her shoulder. "Why are you giving this to me?"

"I need you to get in your car and drive to 44th Street. You're going to speak in my place at today's meeting."

Hannah shook her head. "No. I can't."

"You will."

"Please don't do this to me."

Claude closed his laptop. "I advise you to leave now to make sure the event planners have everything in place, and that the catering service isn't late this time." He headed for the door.

"Where will you be?"

Claude closed his eyes, swallowing past the lump in his throat. "There's someone I need to take care of." He opened the door and exited the room. The building.

Chapter Twenty-Four

NICK DIDN'T KNOW what he'd gotten himself into. He splashed cold water onto his face until he was numb. With the rushing sound of the faucet, he couldn't hear the rattling of his chains. He didn't dare look because it made his body hot with anger every time.

How could Claude chain him up like a fucking slave?

His only saving grace was that Claude had left enough for him to move freely around the bathroom, though he couldn't reach the door. There was nothing he could use as a weapon either. Nick had searched the cabinets for anything to help him get free, but besides a few bottles of bodywash and shampoo, nothing. Not even a single razor blade to keep on him for when Claude returned.

Nick dragged himself to the bathtub and squatted on the temperate marble floor. He stared at the empty plate next to his foot. Claude had left hours before, and Nick had gotten hungry. So he ate—though he wanted to vomit—and preserved his strength in case he needed it. With Claude, he couldn't tell what his next move might be. The guy was unpredictable. A wild card. Nick dropped his head onto his raised knees.

Eric had been right all along. Claude was crazy, and Nick was an idiot for not seeing it in the first place. If he got out of there, he was through with Claude. For good.

The bathroom door opened, and Claude stepped inside. His gaze immediately fell onto the plate. The relief on his face was unmistakable. "You ate. That's good."

Nick bit back a retort, though he desperately wanted to hurt the man standing in front of him. He glared at the towering, imposing figure. "How long do you plan to keep me here?"

Claude took a seat on the edge of the Jacuzzi bathtub. His eyes never wavered. "That depends on you. You know that. Now..." Claude leaned in close. "Are you ready to talk?"

"Yeah. Let's talk about how fucking crazy you are. Is that the real reason why Christian left you? Because you're psychotic?"

Claude's expression didn't change. He sat there staring at Nick, his lips compressed and brows furrowed, concentrating.

Nick growled. "The real Christian is *dead*. He didn't leave you a year ago. He went missing. Police searched for months, but nothing ever turned up. No body. No evidence. Dude just disappeared without a trace. He's dead, and I know you had something to do with it, you delusional prick."

Without a word, Claude headed for the door.

Nick bit his lip, his fists clenched tight. He'd expected Claude to do something. Be angry. Yell. Hit him. Anything. But the calmness pissed him off. "Claude."

The blond stopped but didn't turn around.

"Did you really kill that guy? The one chasing after me?"

Claude glanced at him over his shoulder as he pulled open the door, his eyes dark and hardened. His face was grim.

Nick swallowed as he studied his features. It was true then.

"We'll talk later." Claude closed the door shut.

FOUR DAYS HAD passed since he'd woken up chained in the bathroom. Nick didn't have a clue what was going on in the outside world. All he knew was each day Claude brought him his food and clean clothes. The other day, he even brought some books and a portable DVD player. They hadn't talked since Nick revealed what Hannah had told him about Christian.

Nick stared across the room at the locked and unreachable window, though he didn't really see it. He thought about Amy and the implied threat to her life. Was she safe? What if another stranger visited her room again, only next time with the intent to kill her? How would he ever fucking know? He thought about his job. The one he probably no longer had since he'd been MIA. Images of Eric clouded his mind, and he hoped like hell the guy checked on Amy every day.

"I need to get the fuck out of here."

By any means necessary.

Claude entered the bathroom with clothes and fresh towels later that night.

Nick observed the man's powerful strides as he crossed the room. He was dressed in his favorite gray cashmere and silk-blend tracksuit pants and matching hoodie, which meant he'd probably just gotten back from the gym. His dark-blond locks were slightly plastered to his sweaty forehead. The white tee beneath the sweatshirt clung to him like a second skin, emphasizing his chiseled, lean muscles. Heat spread through Nick's lower body. Despite everything, he would probably always be attracted to him. His body craved the older male.

Claude set the things onto the countertop and moved to leave.

"I'm sorry," Nick blurted.

Claude looked back at him, his posture filled with impatience. "What for?"

"The things I said over the last few days." Nick averted his gaze to Claude's tennis shoes. "I was confused and afraid, I guess."

"There's no need to apologize. I've always forgiven you. I always will." He took a step backward toward the door.

Nick gazed upward, his heart hammering. "Eric was right."

Claude paused, his eyes narrowed as he stared at him without a word. He crossed his arms, waiting for him to elaborate.

"I used to be in a gang. That guy chasing me? Probably sent to kill me." He *had* taken their money and disappeared.

"Why?" Claude asked.

"*Why?*" Nick snorted, his gut churning as memories of a past he'd do anything to forget about haunted him. "I ran away from home when I was fifteen after..."

"After what?"

Nick licked his trembling lips. The room was hot suddenly, and his chest rose and fell with each deep breath he took. The walls seemed like they were closing in on him. He shut his eyes.

"After my father molested me. And my mom didn't believe me when I told her."

Claude didn't say anything.

Nick could hear the blood rushing through his own ears as he continued. "So I left to live on the streets. But I ran out of money I stole from my parents. When I was found by a street gang who wanted me in, I easily said yeah. They wanted me to deliver some packages, and they'd give me a cut. I did it so I could at least buy food. Rent an apartment. Buy whatever else I needed. After I found out Amy had leukemia, I started stealing money from their collections to send to her. It took them a while, but they found out and tried to kill me. So I left. Took the money I had and moved to start over somewhere else. I was about nineteen.

"My parents were dirt poor living in the Bronx, so I knew they couldn't afford Amy's treatments on their own. I knew I needed money fast if I wanted to help my sister, so I started selling sex services online. Mostly blowing guys off for money and overcharging them. Some of my clients paid extra if I did other things. Weird things. I was actually making pretty good money, but I still lived in that shitty apartment because the bulk of it went to Amy."

Nick smirked at Claude's shocked features. "Yeah, not the innocent street kid you thought I was, huh?"

Claude cleared his throat. "When did you meet Eric?"

"I met Eric at Jenkins. Sex work is fucking depressing, so I would always go in there, to the bar, to get drunk on tequila. We talked a few times, and he took care of me. Made sure I got home okay. Sometime later, he helped me get a job there. I quit selling myself afterward, and I got my GED." Nick didn't want to recall how close he'd come to offing himself. Living life as a broken, paranoid whore had depressed him. He'd hated life and could barely stand to look at himself in the mirror without wanting to vomit. Four years of being friends with Eric, doing normal work, had changed him. He still got a little paranoid from time to time, but otherwise he'd moved on without looking back. "Meeting Eric was the best thing that ever happened to me."

"And me?"

Nick peered into Claude's pain-filled features, at a loss for what to say. He opened his mouth to speak, though nothing came out.

Instead of being angry, Claude nodded and moved to the bathtub. He pushed up the stopper and twisted both dials, adjusting the water so that it was hot, but not scorching. "You get bathed here. I'll use the guest bathroom."

Nick abruptly got to his feet, his chains rattling against the marble floor. He bit his lip, trying to rack his brain for any way to keep Claude from leaving. "Stay with me," he said in a low voice, wondering if Claude could even hear him over the rushing water. Nick undid the buttons on his shirt and slid the fabric down onto the floor.

Claude's eyes darkened with lust.

Nick gave him a faint smile. He moved to the sweatpants he wore, untying the drawstrings and pulling them down his thighs before kicking them away. He was commando beneath his clothes.

Claude sucked in a deep breath. His growing erection was obvious behind his tracksuit pants.

Nick approached him first.

That was exactly what he needed.

Claude was hard, but the man still made no move to touch him. Nick sank into the tub, the hot water soothing, yet stifling. He submerged his entire body, the bubble jets tickling his skin, and then came back up to find Claude glued to the spot, his gaze on him.

Nick reached for the pouf and held it out to Claude. "Could you give me a hand?"

Claude took it. He moved closer to the edge of the tub and lathered it with citrus-scented bodywash before pressing it to Nick's left shoulder.

Nick closed his eyes as the soft sponge slid across his skin, almost tentatively. He moaned. Claude massaged the soap into his chest and abs.

"Lower," Nick said. He lifted his hips.

"Christian…"

"Please?" He opened his eyes to see the hesitation in Claude's gaze. The uncertainty. But the yearning was there, too. He wanted this. He was dying to touch him.

Claude released a shaky breath. He hesitantly submerged the loofah into the steaming water, hovering above Nick's semi-erect cock.

Nick tossed his head back with a groan as Claude wrapped it around his dick and bathed him gently. All the negativity from talking about his past vanished, replaced by feel-good endorphins rushing through his body. He snatched the loofah from Claude, so only his hand remained underwater, touching him.

"Don't stop."

Claude wrapped his fingers around his shaft and stroked. Water splashed and made loud waves, but they didn't care.

Nick's balls tightened. He lifted his hips so only the head of his erection bobbed above the water. Stars filled his vision, and he clenched his teeth together as his cum gushed into the tub like a fountain.

"Fuck."

Claude's hand stilled.

Nick kneeled and faced him. His gaze dropped to Claude's lap where his erection strained against his silk and cashmere pants. The front was wet.

"Come here." With his hands on Claude's legs, he guided the older man until they faced one another. He spread Claude's knees apart.

Anticipation played out on Claude's face as he buried his fingers in Nick's damp hair. "I missed you so much."

Nick's hands slid higher. Once he reached his thighs, something hard and small skimmed his palm. Realization dawned on him.

The key to the collar was in Claude's pocket.

Trying not to let it show that he knew, Nick leaned in and kissed him. Claude moaned into his mouth, filling him with the taste of exotic spices. Nick stroked him, ruining his nine-hundred-dollar pants with wet hands. Claude probably couldn't have cared less in that moment.

Nick pulled away first, licking his lips and tasting their mingled essence. "Let's get these off."

Claude only nodded as Nick hooked his fingers into the waistband and slid them down. He also wasn't wearing any underwear. His cock was large and veiny, weeping, and ready to explode. Nick didn't hesitate to lower his mouth to the tip, licking clean a trail of salty precum. It twitched beneath his tongue.

Claude sucked in a deep breath. "I didn't want to do these things, I swear. I never wanted to hurt you, Christian, but sometimes you leave me no choice."

Nick sucked him into his mouth, gradually swallowing inch after inch. While he breathed through his nose and tried not to gag at Claude's sheer size, he groped around Claude's pants, searching for the pocket that held the key.

"You have no idea how much it pains me to see you like this," Claude said.

Not as much as it pains *me to be like this, you dick.*

Claude's grip in his hair tightened. "I don't want you to worry about Amy. After the envelope she'd received, I hired a security detail team to watch over her from afar."

Nick gazed up at him—that incredibly handsome man—filled with awe, terror, and disbelief. Claude's cock spilled from his mouth with a trail of saliva connecting his lips to the tip.

"What? Why did you do that?"

Claude gave a nonchalant shrug. "Because she is important to you, and you are important to me. It's that simple." He brushed his finger across Nick's lips, smearing the moisture. "Now get on your knees. Please."

Nick fidgeted with Claude's pants, suppressing his panic. His gaze never wavered from him, either. "In the tub?"

"Too slippery. You might end up hurt. I want you right here." He inclined his head to the marble floor near the countertop.

Nick slid out of the tub, grabbing the key and fisting it as he got out. Sweet-smelling steam filled the room, and the floors were mild enough to walk on. Nick knelt in front of the double sinks, his body tight with anticipation. He wanted it to be over. For the entire ordeal to be ended that night. Before that, though, he needed Claude inside him one last time. Nick gazed at the floor as he tried to figure out why, but he didn't have an answer. Despite Claude's inability to see the real him; despite Claude violating him; despite being locked up like a wild animal by the man, Nick still craved him as much as the first time Claude had brought him to his penthouse.

Claude stalked toward him, his eyes dark as he shed the remainder of his clothes. He dropped to his knees behind Nick, his strong fingers digging into his hips, heavy erection prodding his entrance.

Nick moaned.

Claude's lips were soft and moist as he pressed them to Nick's shoulder and worked his way down until he landed a passionate one to the base of his spine. "I'll get the lubricant from the—"

"Don't. Don't you fucking stop."

Claude seemed hesitant, but he continued. He skimmed his tongue across Nick's ass, moaning as he tasted his entrance.

Stars filled Nick's vision. He panted hard, wanting badly to grab onto something, but only marble lay beneath him. His arousal grew, and precum dripped onto the floor.

When Claude thrust his hot tongue inside of him, he cried out with pleasure. "Fuck me."

Claude pulled back with a chuckle. "I don't remember you being this crude."

Nick didn't respond. Instead, he braced himself for the initial thrust. He pushed back against Claude's cock, the tip of which pressed against his hole, and took his girth inside of his body.

Claude groaned. "That's it. Take what belongs to you." He squeezed Nick's cheeks, spreading him wider. "I'm yours. Now and forever. Always."

Nick shuddered as Claude filled him completely. He was so large. So hot. His cock pulsed inside him. Nick spread his legs farther apart, even though his knees hurt on the hard floor. He wriggled his hips, hoping to encourage Claude to move already.

Claude pulled out of him gently, then without warning, thrust back in with force. So much that Nick nearly slid across the floor. They moaned in unison. Claude adjusted his position and slammed in and out of him, his hands locked around Nick's hips to hold him steady.

Nick's arms shook with the pressure of holding himself up during Claude's brutal thrusts. They gave out and his cheek hit the marble. He cursed.

Claude wasn't deterred in the slightest. He lifted Nick's hips and continued his hard strokes. "I've missed you...in my bed. In my arms. I've been lonely without you."

Nick shifted his head to the side, ignoring the pain in his cheek.

Claude buried himself so deep then, and his balls touched the backs of Nick's thighs.

Nick whimpered.

Claude leaned over Nick's heated body, interlacing their hands. He rained kisses on Nick's back. "You have no idea how close I came to coming in here and removing the collar. Of bringing you to bed and making love to you all night."

At the mention of the collar, Nick realized he had a chance to unlock the thing himself. He just needed to keep Claude distracted.

"Why didn't you?" he asked, his voice cracking.

"You know why." Claude buried his face between his shoulder blades. "I can't have you leaving me. Not again. I barely survived the first time."

Nick half listened while he used his one hand—the one with the key that Claude hadn't grabbed, thank God—and fumbled around for the keyhole.

"Does that mean anything to you?" Claude asked.

Nick stopped. "I'm sorry. For everything."

Claude didn't respond. Instead, his warmth left Nick's back.

Panic rose in Nick. Did he notice he held the key?

Claude took hold of his hips again and resumed fucking him. This time, his strokes were long and deep. Gentle.

Nick's own cock throbbed with the desire to be touched.

As if reading his mind, Claude took hold of him, stroking in time to his thrusts.

Nick's eyes rolled backward. He dropped the key, but recovered it before Claude noticed. Clenching it tight, he succumbed to the pleasure pouring into him. The bathroom was stifling, the scent of citrus and musk lingering heavily in the air. The erotic sounds of their soft panting and loud moans echoed around the room. Nick's balls tightened.

Claude rocked against him harder and faster. He was getting close. Meanwhile, his deft hand caused all kinds of magic between Nick's legs. He stroked his shaft and pushed the pad of his thumb into his slit. He massaged and squeezed his testicles and outlined his taint.

Nick gritted his teeth hard and squeezed his eyes shut as his orgasm shook him. Unable to hold back, he cried out as he came again in a blinding wave, jets of cum spurting from his cock onto the floor several feet away. Nick's body morphed into jelly, ready to collapse, held up only by Claude's strength.

"Beautiful," Claude whispered, his voice tight and strained. His thrusts grew more erratic and less controlled. "I'm...I'm coming..." A guttural cry escaped him as he filled Nick with hot, thick semen.

Nick shuddered at the still-new sensation. Outside of the last time he'd been with Claude and that very moment, no one had ever come inside him. Not even his own father all those years back. Nick had fought him tooth and nail to ensure that. And afterward, he made sure his clients wore condoms.

Claude collapsed on top of him, his breathing heavily.

Even with Claude still inside of him, going soft, his cum leaked out. Nick shuddered with discomfort.

His own body cooled, and his senses regained, Nick shoved the key into the keyhole at the side of the collar and twisted it open. The metal band fell onto the floor with a loud clang.

Claude pushed himself up. "What was that?"

Without thinking, Nick reared back and head-butted Claude. The older male groaned and fell backward. Nick didn't look back to inspect where he'd hit him. Adrenaline flooded his body. Since he was free, he needed to get the hell out of there.

Claude stumbled to his feet. Nick caught a glimpse of blood pouring from his nose. His flashbulb-wide eyes were filled with shock and emotional pain. Nick didn't dwell on it. He shoved Claude into the tub and slipped on the T-shirt and sweats, not bothering to stop to make sure they were on properly. His one goal: get to the fucking elevator.

Nick flew down the long hallway on dysfunctional legs, crashing into an expensive vase, knocking it to the floor in a million shattered pieces. A picture fell from its niche. Nick didn't stop. He zoomed past the kitchen into the main living room.

Before he could reach the door, Claude grabbed his ankle. Nick barely braced himself as he went crashing to the floor. He winced as his sternum hit the veined marble. Only his face had been protected by his hand.

A soaking wet Claude spun him around, his eyes wild, his teeth bared like a predator about to attack its prey.

Nick kicked at him, but Claude blocked. Nick struggled to get away, but Claude pulled him back. He pinned Nick's body beneath his own and fought to take control of his hands.

"Let me go," Nick shouted. A red haze filled his vision, and he seethed with rage. He fought until his arms hurt, yet Claude didn't budge. He struggled. Each minute that passed, his body became more worn down. His breathing labored as Claude increased the pressure on his chest.

Nick glanced at the door. At the Down button on the elevator that was his key to freedom away from Claude.

Claude wrapped his hands around Nick's throat.

Nick stared into his angry face, eyes widened. Shock filled his body as he realized he couldn't breathe. Instinctively, he reached for Claude's hands, trying to use every ounce of strength he possessed to pry them off. Claude was stronger. More determined. He tightened his grip each time Nick fought. Nick coughed and tried to suck in oxygen, but he couldn't.

Panic overrode his senses. He was going to die... Claude was prepared to kill him to keep him from running away. Warmth spread through his bladder, down his thighs and legs.

Claude screamed at him. "You're not walking out of here, Christian! Not again! You're not leaving me again!"

Nick's eyes bulged painfully. Black spots filled the edges of his vision until he saw only a fraction of his peripheral surroundings. His heart rate slowed. His body seemed to resemble lead. He tried to say something, anything, but only a barely audible squeak escaped him.

Please, God. I don't want to die.

Against his will, Nick's eyes rolled back into his head. Darkness filled his vision.

"Oh, God…"

The vise grip on his throat loosened. Nick sucked in a lungful of air through his bruised esophagus. He coughed and sputtered and breathed. He blinked several times until his vision returned to somewhat normal.

Claude stood over him, his eyes haunted. He stared down at Nick, pale and unmoving, as if he'd seen a ghost.

Nick took advantage of whatever distracted him. He pulled Claude's feet from under him. The man didn't brace himself before he crashed onto the frosted-glass coffee table.

Sheer willpower was the only thing that got Nick to his feet, racing for the elevator. He pressed the button and glimpsed back at Claude lying still among the broken shards, blood pouring onto the floor from somewhere on his body. Nick didn't stop to examine him. He didn't want to. The door dinged open, and Nick hurried inside, pressing the button for the lobby. The doors closed and the metal box descended. Relief filled him.

It was over. It was finally over.

Chapter Twenty-Five

COLD AIR SEEPED through Claude's bones as he peered over the balcony, ignoring the Manhattan skyline in favor of the objects beneath him: luxury cars and a vast array of lights. But no Christian. He chuckled darkly.

"Nick," he corrected.

After all, Christian was long dead.

Claude slumped onto the concrete, eyes unseeing anything else around him. His clothes were dripping wet and clinging to him, and the twenty-degree weather was biting. At the moment, however, he didn't care if he caught pneumonia and died.

He finally remembered what happened to Christian. The *real* Christian. Claude's entire body shook from shock.

It had happened over a year before. The night Christian strutted into his penthouse, dressed in unfamiliar clothing, more expensive than anything Claude usually bought for him.

"I'm leaving you," Christian had said with no remorse in his powder-blue eyes. He'd found another lover, a richer, older businessman who was infatuated with him.

Claude had been devastated. He'd debased himself, begging for his lover—the only light in his otherwise bleak world—to stay with him. He dropped to his knees in front of Christian's thirteen-hundred-dollar Ferragamos.

Instead of the loyalty and compassion he expected from the young man he'd called "lover" for the last four years, Christian merely smirked at his pain.

In that moment, Claude had no idea who Christian was.

"Come on, Claude, you're making me feel bad. Get up. You knew this was about to happen as much as I did, right? Don't get me wrong, I had a great time with you. But it's like the saying, all good things must come to an end." Christian knelt down then, risking his tailored pants getting dirty at the knees. He locked gazes with Claude's, his expression so disgustingly innocent and irresistible at the same time.

"Let's come to an end with a bang," Christian said.

Coming back to the present, Claude shivered atop his balcony as he touched fingers to his bottom lip. He closed his eyes as the memories he'd buried in the recesses of his mind rose once again. Christian had wrapped those lean arms around Claude's shoulders and kissed him like he'd done a thousand times before, with exaggerated passion. Performing, more than enjoying himself. He'd tasted sweet, yet not as exquisite as a Montrachet. No, that night he'd tasted like a low-end wine, the kind a homeless bum could get his hands on.

Claude had ripped his clothes off him, and laid him on the living room floor in the same exact spot he'd struggled with Nick. Claude had slapped him, recalling how much Christian liked to be hurt during lovemaking. Whether it was because of self-imposed guilt at leaving Claude or because it was to be their last intimate night together, Christian took the abuse. He absorbed the aggression Claude forced on him while he fucked him.

Claude tasted his bittersweet skin; inhaled the familiar scent of warm honey and sun-dried grass, mingled with their musk. Christian had been something of a screamer, and the thought of never hearing his lusty moans and cries again had brought out a side of Claude he'd never known existed.

Claude would kill Christian before he allowed anyone else to have him.

At the peak of Christian's orgasm, Claude had wrapped his hands around his throat. Christian hadn't fought him at first. He'd been under the impression Claude meant to help him achieve an incredible orgasm. It didn't take long. Christian had come hard in a matter of minutes. But even after, Claude hadn't let go.

His grip had tightened. Christian's half-mast eyes flew open, and in them, the realization of what Claude meant to do shone bright. He'd fought then, yet to no avail. The more he struggled, the tighter Claude's grip. Claude had stared into those bulging eyes and held down his writhing body, but he'd felt nothing. Not a single emotion filtered through his mind. Nor a single memory of their time together. He'd been on autopilot, his mind filled with white noise and one word, an affirmation: "Mine."

Christian scratched his forearms bloody in an attempt to get free, but he took his last breath beneath him. Claude had remained calm, even afterward, when he'd bundled Christian's lifeless body onto his yacht and dumped him into the Hudson River.

Not until he returned home did he realize what he'd done. The spot in the living room was a mess of Christian's torn clothing, blood, semen, and sweat. Claude had lifted what remained of Christian's shirt and pressed the fabric to his nose, inhaling the crisp scent of brand-new quality clothing, but beneath it, the smell of Christian was so strong, it seemed as if his young lover was still in the room with him. Claude had buried his face in the cloth and wept like he never had. He'd cried for hours before finally calling Hannah—the only person he truly trusted—and told her that Christian was gone. That he'd intended to run off with his new paramour, and now he was gone.

Hannah had assumed he'd meant Christian left with his new beau. He let her believe the lie. The lie he'd convinced himself was true because he could not deal with the consequences of that tragedy.

In the present, Claude dragged himself back inside. He skimmed through the carnage that was his living room. The shattered coffee table and broken vase. The upturned picture. The blood that appeared thick and dark against his black marble floors. He touched his scalp, wincing at the tenderness. His fingers were coated in the sanguine fluid. He'd been cut open, but the wound was superficial. He would stop bleeding soon enough.

He eyed the spot on the floor where he'd held Nick down and nearly strangled him to death.

Nick...

Claude took a deep breath. For over a year, he'd believed that Christian was truly out there somewhere with someone else.

That mistake nearly cost a young man his life.

A young man who'd had nothing to do with Claude, yet still loved him anyway, even when Claude continued to confuse him with his former lover. Bile rose in his throat, threatening to choke him with memories of the things he'd done to him over the last two months. Just remembering his hands around Nick's throat made his stomach roil.

Nick must think him insane. Claude wasn't so sure he wasn't. Sinking to his knees, he prayed to God he would make things right once the opportunity arose. Even if Nick refused to ever see him again.

Chapter Twenty-Six

NICK HOPPED OFF the train once it reached the final stop. He ignored the stares he got from others who gave him a wide berth to get off first. He probably looked like he'd been mugged, what with the bruises and rumpled clothes. Oh, and the fact he wasn't wearing any shoes.

Muggings were common where he came from, but walking through Grand Central Station like that? He was surprised security hadn't stopped him.

Nick dashed out into the cold night air, not minding whatever piss, shit, and trash he stepped on. He jogged down 103rd, cringing at every sound. Every backfiring car. Every heavy footfall on the pavement seemed like it was behind him.

Nick spun around, glancing back at the darkened street he'd just left. No one was chasing him. No one was coming up behind him with the intent to kill. He scrubbed his face and continued the trek to Eric's place. Claude wasn't coming to finish what he'd started.

As he approached Eric's apartment, the blaring Latin hip-hop slowed his steps. Droves of Puerto Rican men spilled from his best friend's apartment and onto the curb. Young men with tats, wearing bandannas, big tees, and baggy pants that didn't hide the fact they were strapping. An angry Taino rapped about Boricua pride.

Nick stopped, his heart pounding hard. Eric was probably just throwing a party, but he knew that atmosphere only too well. The people, the way they talked, the way they moved, what they wore, and the air of menace they gave off... All of it instantly transported him back to his days working under a gang.

Eric wasn't still in one, was he?

Nick changed direction and walked back the way he'd come. He'd return later and talk to Eric alone, maybe. Before he crossed the street, however, Nick hesitated.

Where could he go? Outside of Eric, the only other place was home to his mom, and that shit was not happening, or he could go back to Claude. Just the thought of going back to that insanity made his throat tighten.

Eric was his only hope.

Taking a deep, steadying breath, Nick approached the partygoers. The music got louder, and the sweet, pungent odor of Kush filled his nose. The curb was crowded, but Nick made his way to the front door.

Someone pushed him from behind. "Watch where you stepping, *puta*."

Nick ignored him. Inside, the music was deafening. Men and skimpily dressed women filled every corner of Eric's apartment. Nick squinted from the smoke and haze floating in the air. Bottles of Don Q rum littered the table and floor. He spotted Eric sitting on the couch between a man wearing sunglasses and a snapback, and a Chicana in a skintight dress sipping a coquito. Eric smoked a purple bud through a glass pipe.

Nick approached them. He settled beside the coffee table, on the girl's side, and grabbed his friend's jersey. "Yo, Eric. We need to talk, man. Now."

Eric stared at him with glossy eyes. A slow smile spilled across his mug. "Nicky, bro, what the fuck are you doing here, vato?"

Nick glanced around at all the eyes on him. He swallowed hard, trying not to let his nerves show. These guys were predators. If he showed a weakness, they'd attack him, like a pack of wild animals.

Nick yelled over the music, "I need to talk to you. Let's go outside."

The guy in the snapback looked him up and down. "Who's the gringo?"

Eric turned to the guy with a smile. "That's a real good question, yo. Hold up." He stood on the table and cupped his hands over his mouth. "Yo, Mendes, turn that shit off."

The music disappeared. There were several groans and Spanish swears from the attending. Sweat dampened the pits of Nick's shirt.

Eric, perched high above the others, frowned when he faced Nick again. "What happened to you, bro?"

Nick brought his hand to his throat, trying to shield the bruises from view. The gazes on him were unnerving. "Could I talk to you outside for a minute?"

"What's your hurry, Nicky? You just got here. I haven't even introduced you to my crew yet." Eric stuck out his hand for Nick to take. "Come up here, man."

Nick's gaze narrowed. "I don't want to get on the fucking table, Eric," he said in a low voice.

Eric gave him a lopsided smile. "It's cool, bro." He addressed the others. "Luis asked a very important question just now. Who's the gringo? Well, Luis, let me introduce you to my best friend. Mi hermano. Nick Martin."

Nick peered around at all the faces. Some were curious, some indifferent, while others were perpetually pissed off. He didn't know why, and he didn't plan on sticking around for Eric's charade. Nick backed away, prepared to leave.

"*Sólo una cosa más,*" Eric said. "I forgot to mention. Nick is also the guy who stole money from his former gang *and* sold dope without ever getting caught by the pigs."

Nick spun around to face Eric's smug smile. All traces of friendliness were gone from him. His features were hard. Lines that Nick never noticed appeared on Eric's forehead. Gone was the familiar glint in his dark eyes that Nick had grown accustomed to. His gaze was blank and indiscernible.

Eric hopped off the table and stood in front of Nick, close enough for his hot, pungent breath to hit him in the face. "What? You didn't think I knew?"

Nick didn't respond.

"'Course I knew, B. I make it my business to know who I invite in my circle. In my line of work, you have to."

"What kind of bartender needs to know the personal details of their friends?"

There were a few snickers from the gathered. A few insults.

Eric held his hands up. "Oh, wait, let me re-introduce myself." He made a show of straightening out his jersey as if it had expensive suit lapels. That gained him a few fucking laughs.

Nick wasn't amused.

"I'm Eric Ruiz, and this right here..." He swept his hand around the crowd. "This is Los Gorillas. *Mi familia.* And I'm their *padrino.*"

Nick clutched his fists at his side, his body trembling at the confirmation of his worst fears. He was alone in a room full of thugs. The last time that had happened, he'd narrowly escaped one of the worst beatings in his life. Worse than even his initiation. And to add insult to injury, all of his escape routes were gone. As if sensing his urge to get the hell out, Los Gorillas members blocked off the doorways and windows. He couldn't run. Not this time.

Claude's words came back to haunt him. The guy had warned him about Eric all along, yet Nick had refused to believe him.

"I know you're probably wondering, but let me be clear. Los Gorillas staged the break-in at your house. Los Gorillas visited Amy at the hospital and dropped off that package."

Nick's jaw dropped. He remembered the incidents. The pictures of Amy with blacked-out eyes and crude words written beneath her portrait. Nick's fists tightened. He glared at his *former* best friend, ignoring the stinging pain of blunt nails digging into his palms.

"Did you also send that thug to kill me?"

Eric took back his seat on the sofa between Luis and the chick. "Nah, man. I swear on the Santa María I didn't. LG didn't have nothing to do with that, hermano."

"Don't call me hermano. Not ever again."

Eric shrugged. "Fine by me. Anyway, your old gang caught up with you. They're looking to kill you for whatever you done to them. And those are some bloodthirsty motherfuckers."

Nick swallowed the bile in his throat. He was gonna be sick.

"Don't worry. Los Gorillas sent them a message, loud and clear, to stay off our turf. To keep them off your back. You should be thanking us."

Nick studied Eric's face. His secretive smile. Those eyes filled with hope for something. He crossed his arms, feeling cold all of a sudden. "What do you want?"

"You." Eric observed Nick's features with a chuckle. "I've always wanted you, Nick. NYPD keep busting our peddlers every time we put them on the street. We can't do nothing with those racist crackers breathing down our necks. What we're missing is someone like you. Someone who can sell large amounts of dope undetected. Not gonna lie, we lost too many guys, so we ain't pushing enough product. That's where you come in. We just need you to do what you were doing in your old gang."

Nick shook his head. He raked a sweaty palm through his hair. He'd made a vow never to go back to that life ever again.

Eric arched a brow at him. "No?"

"It won't work. Police will suspect me too."

Eric laughed, and a few others joined him. "You don't get it, do you? You're white. You look like a preppy fucking gangsta-wannabe, vato. Ain't no police suspecting you of anything. But I'll make this easier for you. Amy."

Nick's head shot up, his eyes wide at the mention of his sister's name. The self-satisfaction on Eric's mug said: Got 'im. Nick glared daggers at him.

"You want to keep her safe, yeah? You do this, we leave her alone for good. If you don't...I don't think I need to tell you how badly we're gonna fuck her up."

"You son of a bitch." Nick charged for Eric, but Luis and another guy blocked his way, snarling at him. They reached for their guns.

"What's it gonna be, Nicky? You better answer quickly 'cuz my boys are getting restless. You interrupted their celebration."

"That's it? That's all you need me to do?"

"That's it."

"You sure?" Nick sneered. "Sure you don't want me to change my mind about not wanting to fuck you? I mean, I get it. I turned you down so now you're pissed. Am I right, hermano?"

As Eric's smile fell, his brain probably on overdrive for an equally witty comeback, Nick smirked, enjoying the blowback from his words. Eric didn't know what to say, seemingly unable to stand being under the entire gang's scrutiny. A gang probably questioning their leader's sexuality in that moment.

Nick opened his mouth to say more. Someone's fist flew into his face out of nowhere, landing square on his jaw, sending him reeling. Nick stumbled into the table and landed somewhere near someone's feet. His face throbbed in agony, and he instinctively checked his jaw. It wasn't loose or unhinged, though it hurt like hell.

"*¿Qué carajo haces,* Luis?"

Luis straightened his hat, staring down at Nick as if he hoped to finish what he'd started. "Can't be having this fucking gringo disrespect you, ése. He disrespects you, he disrespects us all." Luis pounded his chest, his gaze locked on Eric.

Nick licked the tangy, metallic blood from the corner of his lip. He got to his feet, instantly swaying. Someone reached for him, but Nick shoved them away. He had eyes for Eric only, letting the rage and pain boiling in his gut show on his face.

"Move, bitch," Eric said to the woman beside him. When she complied, he patted the cushion, urging Nick to sit beside him.

Nick slowly slid onto the couch. He glared at his own hands, folded on top of his lap, knuckles white and aching from the way he held them. He didn't want to see the faces around him, or Eric's triumphant one, lest he be tempted to commit murder.

Eric set a glass in front of him and filled it with the amber-colored liquor. "Are you with us or not?"

Nick stared at the rum. He didn't need to think twice about it. He took the cup and swallowed the biting liquid.

Chapter Twenty-Seven

CLAUDE SWORE AS he left Jenkins' Jazz Bar and marched outside into the bitter-cold air. No one had heard from Nick or Eric. Claude had frequented the bar in the past several days, asking the employees, even the owner himself, but no one had a clue where they might be. Naturally, Claude was in a state of panic, his mind conjuring the worst images of what Nick might be suffering at that moment.

And why wouldn't he be? Eric had obviously lied about his current gang affiliation.

Claude slid into his Ferrari and sped back to his penthouse. He needed to get Eric's address.

Claude didn't take long to reach the skyscraper building he called home. A glistening black Rolls-Royce parked in his designated spot caught his attention. Claude eyed the beast of a machine.

A dark chuckle escaped him. "Of course."

As if on cue, the tinted back window rolled down, and he was met with his father's stern visage. "Get in."

Claude pulled open the door and slid inside. He knew exactly why Augustus had come. During the past few days, Claude had all but neglected his job as COO of Vanderpoel Boating Industries.

Claude pulled the door shut. "I don't have time for this."

Augustus frowned. "What's wrong with you? You look like you haven't bathed in days." He raked his gaze over him with a disgusted sneer. "Is that any way for my son to be seen in public?"

Claude gave him a bored stare, even though his body tensed with anger.

Augustus cleared his throat, unable to bait Claude. "Never mind that. Your loathsome appearance is not the reason I came." He leaned forward, the strong bergamot, sandalwood, and leather scent of his cologne wafting in Claude's nose. "Have you lost your mind?"

"You'll need to be more specific, Father."

Augustus's features twisted in displeasure. "Don't you dare play coy with me. You know exactly what I'm talking about. You think I don't keep tabs on the things you do in my company? I know you've been skipping work and missing meetings. None of that matters as much as you missing our company's annual investors' meeting. How dare you?"

The final three words were spoken with such vitriol, Claude was taken aback. He scanned his father's lined, distressed face, and the ire disappeared from him. Instead, he pitied him. He pitied that his father loved his company more than his own son. His only son. Love for his company had destroyed whatever relationship they might have had.

Just like Claude's love for Christian had ultimately destroyed Nick.

Claude closed his eyes as exhaustion consumed him. He'd barely slept in the past week. "I hereby announce my resignation from Vanderpoel Boating Industries."

"What?"

Claude re-opened his eyes, staring into his father's wide ones. His face was red. Perfect teeth bared. "I'm stepping down as COO."

Augustus shook his head. "No, you're not."

"I am."

"I'll cut you off, do you hear me? I'll make sure you never get a dime from me or your mother."

Claude snorted at the meaningless threat. "I'm a businessman, Father. I stopped needing your money a long time ago."

Augustus jabbed a gloved finger in his face. "You ungrateful wretch. After everything I've done for you, you would leave, knowing the plans your mother and I have?"

Claude knew all about their plans. He would run the company himself so that in two years' time, his parents could retire and spend their final years sailing the world. Then whenever he had children of his own, he would hand over the company to them, same as his father did him, and his grandfather before him. Claude smirked. He definitely didn't feel bad about throwing a wrench in those plans.

"You were micromanaging the company since the day I took over. I'm only giving it back to its *rightful* owner."

"You know the company's always remained in this family."

"Then I suggest you and mother start trying to produce another heir." Whatever child he had in the future, he would not subject him or her to the things his father had with him.

Claude stepped out of the car. He hadn't the energy to continue to argue with him. He was tired, and he still needed to locate Nick. There were things he needed to make right.

Before he could close the door, Augustus stopped him with a hand on top of his. "Where will you go?"

Claude met his terrified gaze, a bitter smirk on his own face. "I have a different path in life." He shut the door and walked away without a single glance back. Making his way inside the lobby, Claude pulled out his cell phone and dialed Hannah's number.

She answered the phone, yet didn't say a word. Her soft, angry breaths were the only indication she remained on the line.

"Congratulations, Hannah. You're the new COO of Vanderpoel Boating Industries. I'll send out the emails on Monday."

Chapter Twenty-Eight

"WHERE'S THE FUCKING money, Nick?"

Nick grinned, ignoring the pain in his split lip. He tossed the bags of heroin at Eric's feet. "Sorry, bro."

With a growl, Eric lashed out, punching him in the jaw and kicking his already sore ribs. "You didn't sell shit today either?"

Nick spat blood. "No one wants to buy drugs from a white guy. They think I'm a cop."

"Fuck!"

As Eric ranted in Spanish, Nick couldn't help smiling. Everything hurt, but Eric was pissed off, thanks to himself. Since he'd reluctantly become Eric's mule, he hadn't sold a single damn kilo of anything. His words were true. Every time he hung out between 116th and 125th Street, people eyed him with suspicion. Not even the junkies who loitered around Pathmark would buy from him.

Nick limped to the bathroom, trying hard not to keel over from the sharp pain in his side. Every breath hurt. He'd been stuck with Eric and Los Gorillas for the last four days, his hope of ever leaving gradually fading. Since he'd gotten there, he'd endured beatings from the members, namely Eric and his right-hand man, Luis. He'd been beaten for fighting back. Beaten for trying to go to the police. And beaten for refusing to sell.

Nick splashed tepid metallic-tasting water into his mouth and onto his face. He winced at the stinging pain. Nick stared at his reflection in the tiny cracked mirror. His jaw was swollen and bruised. His left eye black and purple. Lip cracked and dry. His eyes bloodshot from sleeping with them open. He kept expecting Eric to kill him. But each day that passed with him still alive—at times wishing he wasn't—shocked him to the core.

The door opened, and Luis stumbled inside, hands working to unzip his pants. "Don't mind me, gringo." Luis gave him a lopsided smile before taking a piss in the toilet with a sigh of relief.

Nick turned away in disgust.

"Aw, what's wrong, *ése?* I thought you liked dick. Fucking *maricón.*" He waved his cock in Nick's direction. "Why don't you get down and suck it, since you like dick so much."

Nick gave him a droll glare. "Sounds to me you're the one who actually likes it, faggot."

Despite the sunglasses, Nick knew Luis was pissed. Eric's main stooge zipped himself up and approached Nick. Without warning, he pulled his gun out, pointed at Nick's face. "You wanna say that shit one more time?"

Nick stared at the business end of the Five-seveN without flinching. They weren't gonna kill him. They'd had plenty of opportunities to do so. Luis wasn't gonna wound him either. Not if he wanted Nick back on the streets, pushing their dope. He *might* pistol-whip him, but Nick was already so used to the pain, the thought of more didn't faze him.

Before Luis could decide what to do, a commotion sounded outside the bathroom. A lot of screaming and Spanish insults. The voices moved away, outside.

Luis spun Nick around and shoved him toward the door. He dug the barrel of his pistol between Nick's shoulder blades. "Get out."

Nick twisted the knob and pulled it open. The front door to Eric's apartment had been left gaping. Eric and two of his goons surrounded someone, but he didn't know who, nor could he make out what they were saying from his position.

Luis shoved him to the entryway, though Nick easily went along, placing one foot in front of the other, his heart hammering with dread.

"I told you if I ever saw you again, I'd make you pay." It was Eric's voice.

A solid hit followed his words, along with the thud of someone hitting concrete. A few Ric Flair-esque "woos" came from the two with him.

As Luis forced him outside into the brisk night air, Nick finally saw who'd taken the punch. Claude.

Claude met his gaze from where he lay on the ground. He didn't smile, frown, or say a single word. Just stared at him.

A thousand emotions coursed through Nick as he raked his gaze over Claude. Relief filled him, though he clutched his fists with anger. His palms were sweaty, and his breathing rate increased as Eric circled him like a vulture. He couldn't help noticing that Claude looked like absolute shit. Face haggard and unruly with a beard; hair greasy and unkempt; hazel eyes bloodshot yet laser-focused. He looked nothing like the man Nick had first met what seemed like forever ago.

Eric drove another fist into Claude's jaw, bringing the attention back to himself. "You came to rescue your little *amigo íntimo,* huh?"

Blood trickled down Claude's mouth, but still his gaze never wavered from Nick's. "Christian is dead. I killed him."

Nick's heart sank to the pit of his stomach. He gawked at Claude with disbelief. When Nick had said those words, he'd only meant to piss Claude off. He didn't actually believe Claude had killed Christian, given how insanely crazy he was about the guy.

"I couldn't handle his death. I wanted to forget, so I did. It wasn't until I saw you that I was reminded of him. You're nothing alike, you and Christian, but you reminded me of him so much. I prayed you were really him. That we could be together once more. I would not accept that you weren't Christian, even though I noticed the discrepancies." Claude sat up. Wiped his lips. Unshed tears shone in his eyes, noticeable even from where Nick stood. "I'm sorry, Nick, for the things I've done to you."

Nick looked away, unable to meet his sincere gaze. He wanted to hate Claude. To classify him as a nutjob and be done with him forever. But seeing him like that... Nick squeezed his eyes shut tight, trying not to notice the man's silhouette behind closed lids.

"I promise to make things right."

"Shut the fuck up, *culo.*"

Nick opened his eyes as Eric kicked Claude. The other two joined in, filling the space with their grunts and insults while they stomped and punched Claude to the ground.

Nick tried to squirm away from Luis's grip around his shoulders, but Luis pressed the gun in harder against him. "Stop!"

No one listened to him.

Claude lay on the ground, helpless and balled up, trying to protect his head and middle from the blows being rained down on him. His face was cut open, drops of blood painting the curb.

Nick's heart raced with adrenaline. He needed to do something quickly. He dropped his weight backward and prayed to God that Luis wouldn't accidentally or intentionally shoot him.

They fell onto the pavement hard, with Luis letting out a huge *oomph* as his back took the bulk of the impact.

With no time to think, Nick scrambled to his feet and took off.

"*Qué chingados,* Luis! Go get him, *pinche idiota!*"

Nick didn't look back to see how far or close Luis was. He ran for his life, flying past dilapidated buildings coated with graffiti and small specialty markets in a blur. Cold air filled his lungs, making it harder to breathe, but his legs were on autopilot at the highest level.

He veered left on Lexington Avenue when the first shot rang out close to him. "Shit!" He raced down the street, hoping the cover of darkness protected him from the rapid-fire bullets. Luis let off what seemed like a hundred rounds in mere seconds.

Nick ducked behind Moustache Pizza, his heart ready to explode from his chest. The 23rd Precinct police department was only a few minutes away on foot. The street was quiet except for his panting and Luis's nearby footfalls. The bastard would get too close if he didn't move.

With a big leap of courage, Nick left his hiding spot and bolted down East 102nd, flying past the Shell gas station and a laundromat. Hope filled him. The police department was in sight.

He didn't hear Luis's footsteps behind him anymore, but Nick didn't stop. Not until he threw open the doors and barged inside the brightly lit space. Nick stumbled to the desk, though no one sat behind it. Uniformed and plainclothes officers walked by, some looking really busy, while others sipped coffee from Styrofoam cups and conversed amongst themselves. Impatience rode him. He thought about Claude, and how he'd left him there, being jumped. Eric would kill him if he didn't hurry. Even though Nick disliked the guy right then, he didn't want him dead.

Nick leaned over the empty desk and cupped his hands over his mouth. "There's a guy with a cop killer, and he's shooting at people."

CLAUDE LAY SUPINE on the cold, hard ground, staring up at the pistol barrels pointed at his face. The metallic taste of blood lingered in his mouth. The same sticky wetness clung to his nose—definitely broken—and his head. His ribs ached. Taking in adequate oxygen was an impossible task. One of the thugs had caught him in the balls with his foot, the main reason for his incapacitation. However, he didn't perceive the physical pain so much as he did the emotional one.

Nick had gotten away.

Claude's plan to distract Los Gorillas long enough for Nick to escape had worked. He'd gone in, willing to trade his well-being for Nick's. Nick—the young man who was undoubtedly not Christian. Claude wanted to cry at the truth: he would never see Christian again in that life. He forced himself not to think of that. To focus on the situation at hand. Nick had escaped. Things would be all right.

Then the gunshots rang out, loud and clear, in rapid-fire mode. Claude counted nineteen rounds fired off within a five-second span. Dread clouded his heart. The chances of Nick escaping unscathed were next to impossible.

Eric's amused snort brought Claude back into the moment. "Sorry I gotta kill you, bro. But don't worry. I'll take care of Nick." He swept his hand around the carnage that'd just taken place. "This shit? Nick will eventually forgive me for it. He's good like that. But you..." His dark eyes became shadows, made even more menacing due to Eric's maniacal grin. "You'll never get to be forgiven. You're gonna go to your grave with that regret on your shoulder, as well as the knowledge that it's gonna be me fucking Nick every night from now on."

Claude gritted his teeth. A red haze filled his vision.

"*Buenas noches—*"

"Eric!"

Claude and the others shifted sideways to see the Latino who'd chased Nick run toward them. He'd lost his glasses, and his dark eyes shone with fear.

Eric kept his gun trained on Claude. "Where's Nick?"

"We gotta go. Cops are coming. That fucking bitch escaped, man. Went into the 23rd Precinct. We gotta get the fuck out of here."

Eric glared in his direction, but Luis had already taken several steps backward. "Not until we waste this prick."

"Fuck him. We need to leave now."

"Luis—"

"Victor lied to us, vato. We get locked up, we're screwed. Ain't no LGs on the inside." Luis took off before Eric could stop him.

No one paid Claude any attention.

Taking advantage of the distraction, Claude reached for his pants leg and quickly removed his Walther P22 from its ankle holster. He cocked it. Before any of them were the wiser, Claude fired three precision shots. Two were low on the abdomen. The last one hit the chest.

Three simultaneous groans of agony rent the air. They would live. One not for long.

Claude pushed himself to his knees, taking a deep steadying breath as the world spun momentarily, blackness almost consuming him. He pushed himself to his feet with difficulty. Claude kicked aside their weapons, dropped and forgotten in favor of pain. Everyone except Eric, who struggled to keep his unsteady grip on the pistol. Claude snatched it from him. He glared at Eric, attempting to convey the entirety of his wrath within the depths of his stare.

Unnerved, Eric spat blood in his face. "Go ahead, *hijo de puta,* go ahead and kill me. Nick will never forgive you."

"It doesn't matter." Nick would never forgive him anyway. Not after everything he'd done. The least he could do was rid the neighborhood of the violent scum who planned to sell him out and shoot him.

Claude pointed the P22 to Eric's trembling visage. His mind went blank except for the white noise, distancing himself from the scenario. "From this range, I won't miss."

Eric spat more blood, his blanched mien betraying his agony. His fear. His gaze was hard as he stared down his own death. "Shoot me. Shoot me, mother—"

Claude pulled the trigger and a red hole appeared between Eric's eyes.

A shrill scream from one of the thugs filled the air. He prayed in Spanish and attempted to crawl away, but Claude pointed the gun at him, his finger looming close to the trigger. "Don't."

"Please, please, don't kill me. I got a little girl, yo. *Mi mujer* just gave birth two weeks ago."

Approaching sirens pulled Claude out of that blank space. The flashing lights stung his eyes. Police jumped out of their cars with drawn pistols pointed directly at him. "Drop the gun now," they yelled.

"Help me!" the thug on the ground called. "This guy's crazy. He shot Eric!"

Claude complied with the police officer's orders. He held his hands up and calmly backed toward the closest cruiser so they could put him in handcuffs.

Nick exited a squad vehicle as Claude was arrested and read his Miranda rights. Claude barely listened. He stared at Nick, relief washing over him at the sight of him unharmed. Nick opened his mouth to speak but closed it, as if to say something then would be counterproductive.

A young male cop approached Nick. "Was this the guy?" He pointed in Claude's direction.

Claude's chest tightened.

Nick stared at him, his eyes darkened, almost appearing black. "Yeah. That's him."

Claude took a deep breath, letting go of all the tension in his body. Strangely enough, no malice or anger filled him as he was searched and then ushered into the police car and shut inside. If that was the vengeance Nick chose to seek in retribution for the terrible things Claude had done to him, then he would let him have it. Hell, he deserved it. Pale blond hair and bright eyes filled with hopes and dreams entered Claude's mind.

"Christian..."

He'd robbed that young man of the future he'd deserved. Even if he'd shared that life with someone other than him, Claude had no right to kill him.

He glanced out the window at Nick, grimacing as he turned away from Eric's dead body. He thought of those forest-green eyes, so tormented, even when he smiled. Nothing at all like Christian. This one—that dark, tortured soul who'd never known love—would have stayed by Claude's side had he not ruined what they had with his own brand of insanity. Had he not tried to destroy him too.

Claude cleared his dry throat, craving a cigarette.

"Call the coroner. I'm gonna take this one to the station. Put him in lockup." The officer who'd handcuffed him got behind the wheel and drove away from the scene.

Claude stared outside the window, at the chaos, at Nick being interviewed by other officers. Nick seemed weary and hurt. His body language portrayed both resentment and sadness.

Their gazes met.

Nick gave the barest of headshakes, as he placed the blame squarely on Claude's shoulders.

Claude gladly accepted the weight. "I promise to make this right." He stared back as Nick watched him until neither could see the other anymore.

Chapter Twenty-Nine

NICK SAT IN the corner of Amy's room at the New York Med as Dr. Thompson checked his sister's vitals. He didn't say anything. Couldn't. Hadn't been able to, despite coming to the hospital every day for about a week.

"Everything looks good. I'll get her discharge papers ready."

Nick nodded, glad that Amy got to go home that day.

Julie gave his arm a soft squeeze before heading outside.

Left alone, Nick stood, Amy's coat and things in hand. "Let's get this on you."

Amy didn't say anything as he helped her dress in her sweater, coat, hat, and gloves. His sister should have seen the news about Eric's death. She probably believed that was the real reason why Nick was upset. Nick let her think that. He didn't want her to figure out the man who'd befriended them four years prior had threatened to kill her.

"Nick. There's something I need to tell you."

Nick gazed into Amy's eyes, steely with resolve. "What?" he asked, struggling to keep his voice from cracking.

"It's about Mom. The day she came here to see you."

Nick sighed. "Aims, I don't really want to—"

"Just listen, okay?" She grabbed his hand, gripping it between her two small ones. "You both thought I was sleep. But, I wasn't. I mean, I was at first, but the pain woke me in time to hear the two of you talking. I pretended to be asleep so I could listen in."

Nick's eyes widened. He tried desperately to remember everything he'd said that day. "What?" He moved to pull away, but Amy held onto him, her grip surprisingly strong.

"I heard what you said about Jesse. And Mom..." She glanced at him, her eyes, identical to his own, glistening with tears that spilled down her pale cheeks. "Nick, I'm so sorry."

Nick's heart sank at her cracking voice.

"I've cried so many nights, thinking about what our *father* did to you. I can't even imagine—"

"Aims," Nick pleaded. He had no desire to be reminded of what that bastard had done. There was already enough shit going on in his head, and he had no room for Jesse or his past.

"I'm sorry." Amy let go briefly to wipe her eyes and reddening nose. When she met his gaze again, hers had hardened. "But there's something I need to clear up. Mom lied to you."

Nick hesitated. "About what?"

"She told you Jesse was in jail for rape. That's not true. He's in jail for *attempted* rape."

"Attempted?"

Amy didn't say anything, but the sudden pain in her gaze spoke volumes.

Nick sank onto the edge of her bed, his mouth open, eyes wide with horror. "Please no. No, God, no." White spots clouded his vision. He clutched the sheets until his knuckles ached. The image of his frail sister swam as he stared at her. "He didn't. That sick fucking bastard didn't—"

Amy reached for his hands again, shaking her head profusely. "He didn't. He tried to, Nick. It was the scariest thing I've ever experienced, but he didn't get a chance to. Mom saved me."

Nick gaped at her in disbelief.

A small smile spread across Amy's face. "She heard Jesse come in late one night and head straight for my bedroom. I was supposed to be asleep, but I was in too much pain to relax. Jesse came into my room, drunk and reeking of alcohol. He closed the door behind him. Then he started to..." She swallowed visibly. "He took off his belt. Said he would help me take my mind off the pain."

Nick tightened his grip on Amy's hand. "I'll kill him."

"You won't need to. I'm okay. He didn't touch me. Before he could get his zipper down, Mom flew into the room with a broom. I'd never seen her so angry before. She started beating him with it, yelling that she wouldn't let him take another one from her. He barely got the chance to defend himself. His face was a mess. At one point, he got pissed off and snatched the broom from Mom, but when he tried to hit her with it, I jumped on him, biting, scratching, and punching." Amy giggled. "We wore him down. He finally got tired and left, and that's when she called the police. Told them what happened." Her face sobered. "Mom held me all night, crying and apologizing. She wouldn't let me go for anything. Even when I had to use the restroom, she insisted on following me."

Nick released a shuddering breath as his sister's words sank in. Nicole had actually stopped Jesse for once? A part of him wanted to hate her for giving Amy the protection he'd desired for himself, though he commended her for having the courage to stand up to that asshole. And not a moment too soon from what she'd told him.

"When did all this happen?"

"Six months ago."

"Why didn't you tell me sooner?"

Amy shrugged. "I didn't want you worrying over nothing. I'm okay. Mom's okay. And Jesse's locked up for the foreseeable future. Life is good." She winced. "Well, life *will* be good if you ease your grip on my hand."

"Sorry." Nick let go of her. He thought about Nicole, about the tears she'd shed the last time they'd talked, and the words she'd spoken: "I'm trying." Nick raked a hand through his hair. "If Mom's trying, then I can, too, right?"

Amy's eyes widened. "You really mean that?"

"Yeah, I guess."

Without warning, Amy jumped into his arms. He barely caught her slight frame.

"Thank you, thank you, thank you," she chanted.

Nick wrapped his arms around her bundled-up body, inhaling her sweet cinnamon scent. She'd always naturally smelled like cinnamon, even as a kid. "Our relationship won't change overnight," Nick said, "but I am willing to speak with her again. For you."

Amy nodded. "You promise you won't try to take me away from her?"

Nick gave her a dark grin. "You heard that, too?"

"Yes."

"I promise I won't try to take you away. Though you'll be eighteen in two years anyway, and then I can force you to come live with me and no one can do anything."

Amy popped him in the ribs.

He actually winced from the force behind it. "Ow. Where is all this strength coming from?"

She beamed at him. "I work out when I can, you know. Julie suggested I do some yoga. I even do push-ups when I'm alone in my room."

"You know better than—"

A soft knock sounded on the door.

Nick frowned. Usually, hospital staff knocked once and waltzed right in. Whoever was on the other side waited patiently. Nick moved Amy behind him. "Who is it?"

"Hannah Aldridge. I used to work for Claude."

Nick's stomach did cartwheels at the mention of his name. Over the past week, he'd tried his hardest not to think about that man. He'd moved back into his crappy apartment and tried to forget him.

It'd been impossible.

Every night, Claude haunted his dreams. He'd gone back to work at Jenkins'—probationary of course—but focusing was hard when he kept expecting Claude to show up in his Ferrari, waiting in a darkened corner to take him home. The only time thoughts of Claude didn't consume him was whenever he visited Amy. He'd been visiting her a lot lately.

"Who's Hannah?" Amy asked.

"She's Claude's assistant. Why she's on this side of town, I don't know."

Another swifter knock on the door. "Nick? Are you seriously not going to let me in?"

Nick sighed. Might as well get it over with. "Yeah, come in."

The door swung open, and the blonde beauty strutted inside, impeccable as always in a designer jumpsuit, fur shrug, and spiked heels. She held a manila envelope in her carefully manicured hands.

"Claude said I would find you here," she said without preamble. Her expression softened when she noticed his sister. "You must be Amy. Claude mentioned how beautiful and intelligent you are. I'm Hannah."

Amy stepped forward, taking her proffered hand. "Nice to meet you. I love your outfit."

"Thank you. I got this romper from Saks, actually."

Nick cleared his throat before she started a passionate conversation about clothing. "What are you doing here? In case you haven't realized, I don't have anything to do with Claude anymore. Sounds like you don't, either."

Hannah actually looked saddened by that. "I know, and I'm sorry. But I have something for you." She held out the folder. "I may not work for Claude anymore, but he's still my friend. He asked me to give this to you since he couldn't. Here."

Nick hesitated. He really didn't want to take it, but curiosity and the impatience on Hannah's mug influenced his decision. He took the folder. "What's in it?"

"Why don't you open it and find out?"

Nick opened the folder. A slip of paper with the words Fixed Assets Transfer Form printed across the top glared back at him. Nick blinked twice before skimming the document. There was a list of assets under the description part of the table. The address to Claude's penthouse, the address to his villa in Montego Bay, the Bentley, and the yacht. In the far right, Nick's name was written in for each item under New Custodian/PI. Nothing had been written for Reason for Transfer, but Claude's name was signed and dated.

Nick frowned. "I don't understand."

"Read the next one," Hannah urged.

He flipped the page, finding another important-looking piece of paper. That one had Account Transfer Form across the top. It was more complex and spanned several pages of instructions. Nick scrolled down until he found his name listed under Receiving Account Information. Someone had already filled in his bank account number and social security number. Beside it, listed as Account Being Transferred was Claude's account number and personal details. The entirety of the account was checked to be transferred. Nick leafed through some more, until he got to the Cash Transfer Amount.

The folder slipped from his fingers at the dollar amount being given to him.

"Hey." Hannah bent down and retrieved the paperwork. She waved it in his face. "Do you realize how valuable these pieces of paper are?"

Nick folded his arms across his chest. "What is this, Hannah?"

Hannah arched a perfect brow. "Did you not read the documents? Claude is leaving everything to you."

"Why? If he's hoping to buy my forgiveness, it won't work."

She frowned. "I don't think that's what he's trying to do. He wants to make sure you and your sister are cared for. I spoke with him yesterday. All he talked about was you. He was worried about you and wanted to make sure everything went smoothly so that you could legally get everything. He loves you, Nick."

Nick snorted. "He loves Christian. Or the memory of him, at least. He never even saw me."

"That's not true. His thing with Christian was more of an obsession, really. The actual truth was that Christian made him unhappy. But you..." She jammed a finger in his chest. "I never saw him beam the way he did when he was with you."

Nick forced his breathing to remain slow and steady while memories filtered through his mind. Memories of the good times together. The yacht ride to the Statue of Liberty for the first time. Their trip to Jamaica. The many dates where they actually enjoyed each other's company.

He took the folder and scanned the documents again. "I don't know what to do with this."

"Go spend it all. Take a trip with your sister. Show her the world. Go on a shopping spree." She winked at Amy. "You'd love that, wouldn't you?"

Amy smiled softly.

Nick glared at the older woman, wanting to tell her that Amy, physically, wouldn't be up for too much travel. But he didn't want to embarrass or discourage his little sister.

Hannah gave him a knowing smile. "Claude has the most renowned doctors on call. Don't worry about your sister's treatment. She'll be taken care of. Besides, I hear the Jamaican sunshine does wonders for ailments."

"Jamaica?"

Hannah huffed. "Yes. Jamaica. The truth is, Claude asked me to come here to take you and Amy to Montego Bay. He's worried for your safety after everything that happened, so he wants you to lay low for a few weeks. I was hoping I wouldn't have to go back to him with bad news."

Nick scoffed. "He expects me to up and leave last minute like this? What about my job?"

"You're rich now."

"And Amy?"

Amy grinned. "I've always wanted to visit the Caribbean."

Hannah clapped her hands together. "There you have it. A car's waiting outside to take you to the airport."

"You realize how inconvenient this is?"

Hannah gave him a bored stare. "You realize how difficult you're being? Just think of it as a vacation. You and Amy enjoy yourselves until things die down here."

Nick exhaled a deep breath. She was right. He hadn't had time to take a breather or to even process things fully. Luis was still out there. So was Nick's old gang, according to Eric. He definitely could use a vacation. He glanced back at Hannah, not sure what his expression showed, because her features instantly softened with sympathy.

"Will I see him again?" he asked, voice so low he wasn't even sure he'd spoken.

"Of course. Expect to see him sooner than you think."

Nick gave her a bitter smile. If Claude was truly sorry, maybe they could start over. Get to *really* know one another without Christian in the way.

Nick scoffed.

Or maybe he should just let Claude rot away in an insane asylum.

"Nick?"

Nick peered down at Amy holding onto his arm, her face plastered with one of the sweetest, most innocent smiles he'd ever seen. His gut churned. Whenever she did that, she usually wanted something.

"Amy."

"Can we go to Jamaica? I really want to visit."

He raked a hand through his hair, and finally nodded. "Why not?"

Amy's smile widened. "Can Mom come with us? Please?"

Nick paused. "You're pushing your luck, Aims. Besides, we don't even have a passport—"

"Already taken care of."

Nick glared at Hannah and her smugness.

"What? Claude figured you might want to invite your family. He made passports for Amy and Nicole just in case."

Nick tsked in annoyance. "Fine. She can come."

As Amy jumped for joy, and Hannah celebrated with her, Nick's strength dissipated. He didn't know how it would work out—him and Nicole stuck together for several weeks. But he would try, like he promised Amy.

Images of the blond-haired, hazel-eyed man filled his mind. All of it was possible because of him.

Yeah, he owed it to Nick to be so *generous,* but he didn't have to. Not really.

Nick finally had the means to not only take care of Amy's expenses, he could also show her the world, too. Give her things she'd only ever dreamed about. He could take her and Nicole out of New York and move somewhere far away from the past and anything that reminded them of the painful years they'd spent there.

Nick stared up at the ceiling. Past it. Maybe God had listened to him, after all.

He thought of Claude with a fond smile. Nick looked forward to seeing him again. Maybe not right away, but sometime in the near future.

He draped an arm around Amy's shoulder. "Let's go surprise Mom, then."

Amy beamed brighter than a star as she regarded him. "You really mean that?"

Nick nodded and pulled her toward the door. "I do. For real." He grinned. "Let's go to Jamaica!"

About the Author

Theophilia St. Claire is an up-and-coming author who loves to explore everything dark, taboo, psychological, and gay in her fiction. The more uncomfortable, the better. On the bright side, however, she enjoys romance, anime, yaoi, and laughing at cats. She lives with her family somewhere in the South and is currently on a journey to becoming a bestseller.

Email: theost.claire@gmail.com

Facebook: www.facebook.com/theostclaire

Twitter: @TheoStClaire

Website: www.theophiliamuse.wordpress.com

Also Available from NineStar Press

Connect with NineStar Press

www.ninestarpress.com

www.facebook.com/ninestarpress

www.facebook.com/groups/NineStarNiche

www.twitter.com/ninestarpress

www.tumblr.com/blog/ninestarpress